ALSO BY NINA LEVINE

Storm MC Series

Storm

Fierce

Blaze

Revive

Slay

Sassy Christmas

Illusive

Command

Havoc

Sydney Storm MC Series

Relent

Nitro's Torment

Devil's Vengeance

Crave Series

All Your Reasons

Be The One

Standalone Novels

Steal My Breath

Her Kind of Crazy

USA TODAY BESTSELLING AUTHOR

NINA LEVINE

Published by Nina Levine

authorninalevine@gmail.com
www.ninalevinebooks.com

Editing by Hot Tree Editing
Cover Design ©2016 by Romantic Book Affair Designs
Cover photography Wander Aguiar
Cover model Jase Dean

To Jodie & Becky.

I couldn't have done this one without either of you.

Chapter One

Devil

The only good thing about the January heat in Sydney was the female skin on display. Skimpy shorts, bikini tops, and tight tanks clung to bodies made for sin. It was a fucking smorgasbord of tits and ass all summer long. And I was staring at the best set of tits I'd ever had the good fucking fortune of laying eyes on. But fuck if I'd make a move on them—the blonde they belonged to looked like the craziest bitch I'd seen in a long time. She stood in the middle of a fucking animal cruelty protest, waving her "Stop Animal Cruelty" placard around while spewing hatred towards whoever she thought was abusing the animals she loved.

Although I was in a hurry to get to the clubhouse, I slowed to dedicate a few minutes to her curves. Didn't matter that I had no interest in her or her crazy protesting ways; it never hurt to admire beauty in whatever form it came. However, as my gaze skimmed over her body, another woman stepped in between us, blocking my view.

Jesus, is the universe trying to cause trouble between King and me today? I should be almost at the clubhouse by now, not standing on a footpath with my dick begging to be let loose.

If I thought the blonde had a set I wanted to get my hands on, this dark-haired beauty kicked that desire up a couple of notches. The minute she opened her mouth and spoke, the knowledge that King would cut my balls off if I were late that morning fled my brain.

I stood transfixed while the crowd surged on the road in front of me listening to her speak. Her voice drew them in as easily as it did me. The only difference being that I had no fucking clue what she said. All I knew was that I needed that voice to whisper dirty shit in my ear as I took her body in every way possible. She had the sexiest damn sound I'd ever heard.

Her loose black T-shirt slid off her shoulder as she waved her arm around while she spoke. I only had a side-on view that didn't give me the best opportunity to appreciate her completely. But it allowed me to admire her tattooed waist when her shirt lifted as she moved that arm around. My gaze drifted lower so I could take in her long tattooed legs and a sweet ass she barely covered with tiny ripped denim shorts.

Fuck, if only every Monday morning began with an animal protest in one of King's Cross's streets, led by this dark-haired beauty.

The buzz of my phone ringing distracted me. Without taking my eyes off her, I held it to my ear. "Yeah?"

King's voice snapped into the phone. "Where are you?"

"I'm on my way. I've just left home." I still had an hour before the time he'd set. At the rate I was going, though, I'd be lucky to make it.

"Make a detour on the way, brother. I need some shit from the supermarket, and I need you to drop it off at my place before you come here."

Fuck.

No way in hell would I have time to do all of that before the meeting. I'd give it a good fucking shot, though. "Text me what you need."

He ended the call, and a minute later, his text arrived. I scanned his list. Weirdest fucking shit King had ever asked me to get him—water cracker biscuits, lemons, ginger tea, pretzels and ginger ale. I figured it must be for Jen.

The fact he was looking after Jen was some of the strangest shit around. I hadn't been a member of Storm when they'd first got together so I didn't know what their relationship was like in the early years, but the last year of it had been hell. And not just for the two of them. King had brought his own personal hell to the club; we'd all suffered through it. I wondered what had possessed him to allow a woman who'd left him for another man back into his home.

I watched the dark-haired beauty for another long moment. I dragged that time out for as long as I could, but knowing that King wanted me to drop stuff off for Jen kicked my ass into gear. I'd seen the way he held her yesterday, and I was sure of one thing—he'd cut my balls off for being late to a club meeting, but what he'd do to me for not getting this shit to Jen as soon as possible was unpredictable. And an unpredictable King wasn't something I was willing to take a gamble on.

As I turned to leave, the crowd surged again, and the woman who'd held my attention crashed into me. I saw her coming and held out my arms to catch her.

"Fuck!" she yelled as she attempted to ease out of my hold. She wasn't yelling at me, though, but rather at the man who'd shoved her into me. "You filthy piece of scum," she spat at him. Hell, if her voice captivated me before, it all-out fucking turned me on after that.

Nothing better than a woman with some fight.

Although she clearly wanted me to let her go, I didn't. The menacing glint in the eye of the guy she yelled at concerned me. Lowering my mouth to her ear, I said, "How about you let me deal with him while you get back to your protest?"

Spinning around in my embrace, her brown eyes met mine and I instantly knew I'd found myself a spitfire. No fucking way would she listen to me. Those eyes flashed determination. "How about you let me go so I can take care of this asshole by myself?"

I couldn't help myself; I grinned. Damn, but I loved a woman who gave it to me like that. I tightened my hold on her. "How about we blow this protest and you let me show you—"

The asshole cut into our conversation when he grabbed her shirt and tried to pull her away from me. Anger and a desire to protect her consumed me when he also yanked a handful of her hair, snapping her head back and eliciting a cry of pain from her.

Moving quickly, I let her go and reached for his throat. Wrapping my fingers around it, I squeezed hard enough to ensure he'd struggle for breath. Only a moment passed before he dropped his hold on her and clawed at my hand while gasping.

My teeth clenched with determination. "You want me to let you go, motherfucker?"

Both his hands gripped mine as he fought me, but I didn't ease my hold. He tried to speak, but the only sounds to come from him were grunts because I'd blocked his ability to talk.

"It wasn't a question that required an answer," I said.

"This guy doesn't like to give answers," the woman muttered.

I made a poor judgement call when I turned and glanced at her. The asshole used the opportunity to take a swing at me. The surprise of his fist connecting with my cheek caused my grip on him to loosen, giving him the chance to wedge his fingers between his throat and my hand.

"Fuck," I muttered, getting my head back in the game.

A moment later, my first punch almost knocked him to the ground. My second punch did. He'd chosen the wrong man to fuck with—I didn't earn the name Devil for no fucking reason.

If it hadn't been for someone pulling me off the asshole, I would have continued my assault. However, just as I was getting started, I found myself yanked back and slammed up against the brick fence on the footpath.

I scowled as I met Bronze's eyes. "The fuck?"

Clenching his jaw, he jabbed a finger at me. "Wait here." At my brow lift, he added, "Trust me when I tell you that this shit is the last thing you need to get mixed up in this week. Wait the fuck here."

Without another word, he turned and reached for the dark-haired woman. Snapping his hand around her wrist, he drew her attention and engaged her in a conversation that I couldn't hear over the noise of the crowd. She appeared just as fiery with him as she'd been with me. However, after a minute or so, he managed to get her to agree to follow him back to where I stood waiting.

"Follow me," he barked as he headed towards the side street closest to us.

Following a cop's orders was the last thing I wanted to do, but something in his tone caused me to take heed. I wondered what he knew about the activities Storm had planned for this week. Dealing with Bronze was King's gig; I'd hardly had anything to do with him, so I didn't know how deep in our business he actually was. But I wouldn't have been surprised if he'd been made aware of the shit going down this week. Having the cops on our side would help things run much smoother.

I followed him and the woman to his car parked on the side street. However, when he ordered me to get in the back, I refused. "What the fuck is going on?"

He watched as the woman settled into the back seat before answering me. Stepping close and lowering his voice, he said, "You're going to get in the back. I'm going to drive you away from this shit fight to your bike. And then you're going to head straight to your clubhouse because you'll be needed there in about"—he checked his watch—"an hour or so. Where's your bike parked?"

Before I could answer him, his phone rang. Pressing it to his ear, he said, "What's up?" His face scrunched into annoyance as he listened for a moment. He then said, "I'm on it," and ended the call.

"What's going on at the clubhouse? What the fuck do you know?"

Glaring at me, he appeared to be contemplating something. I knew what that was when he whipped a set of handcuffs from his pocket and snapped them over my wrists. "Get in the car. I have to go deal with another fight that just broke out and then I'll be back to deal with you."

"Fuck! You are fucking kidding, Bronze! I've got shit to do. Just let me go so I can fucking do it."

"Yeah, see the problem with that is I know the chances are high that you'll get yourself involved in another fucking fight along the way with these protesting assholes. And like I said, today isn't a day you need to be getting involved in any shit besides your club shit. So get the fuck in the car and wait for me."

Anger rolled through me. That, and frustration. But I knew when I was down, and I was fucking down. I did what he said and got in his goddam car. He slammed the door closed and left me alone with the dark-haired beauty. At least there was that.

"Arguing with him is pointless," she said, shifting so she faced me with one leg on the seat, her foot tucked under her other leg.

Struggling to keep my eyes on her face rather than all over her body, I said, "You know him?"

"You could say that."

"He's arrested you at one of these protests before?" Not that it appeared Bronze had arrested her, but she *was* sitting in the back of his car, so I wasn't sure what else you'd call it.

She smiled. It lit her whole face up, and my dick jerked his appreciation. Fuck, she was beautiful. Between her big brown eyes, her full lips that were painted in the deepest red lipstick and a face that would cause any man a lapse in concentration, I had to force myself to keep my head clear of the thoughts trying to take over. The kind of thoughts that made me want to reach for her so I could drag those lips to mine.

"He has," she said, jolting me back to the conversation.

"So protesting for animal rights is your thing?"

"It's one of them."

She toyed with a strand of her long hair as she dropped her gaze to my neck and then to my arms. I sat in silence while she checked me out. Who the fuck was I to stop a woman from appreciating what I had on offer? Besides, it drew my attention away from the irritation I felt towards Bronze.

Time passed slowly while we sat there with her eyes on me, or at least that was how it felt. My dick grew so damn hard that I knew I needed to stop her. Usually in this kind of situation, I'd make my move, but sitting in the back of a fucking cop car, restrained by handcuffs, was not the ideal place to do that. So, I went with—"The guy you got in an argument with, you know him?"

Her eyes met mine again. "Yeah. He's a piece of work. Always shows up at our protests and tries to cause problems. We'd have peaceful protests if it weren't for him. He doesn't seem to think it's an issue for animals to be abused so that fucking gambling can continue."

I frowned. "As in greyhounds and shit?" I'd vaguely heard something about the government changing those laws recently.

Her eyes narrowed at me. "Yes, as in greyhounds and *shit*. Tell me, do you know much about what they do to those dogs?"

I fought the grin that wanted to spread across my face. I knew a tiny bit about it, but suddenly I wanted to know every-fucking-thing about greyhound racing and animal cruelty. "Can't say I do. Feel free to enlighten me."

She sat up straighter and leaned forward a little. Her eyes were wide, and her body vibrated with a passionate energy. "The government ran an enquiry into greyhound racing that lasted for thirteen months. They found that over the last twelve years almost a hundred thousand greyhounds were bred and that at least 50 to 70 per cent of those dogs were killed because they weren't competitive anymore. Nearly 70,000 dogs killed, all because of betting. And that's not to mention the horrific cruelty suffered by those animals." Her eyes flashed even wider. "Does that not make you sick? Does that not make you want to do something to help them?"

"Jesus, you should run for office or some shit," I murmured, completely engrossed in what she was saying. Or just in her. I wasn't entirely sure. All I knew was that thoughts of King and Storm had taken a backseat and that wasn't something that ever happened.

She ran her fingers through her hair and relaxed her body. "Fuck that. Those assholes don't do anything unless it benefits them or their friends. I wouldn't be able to bring about real change if I worked for the government."

"So you do these protests often?"

"Every couple of months or so we run one."

"And you think they help bring change?"

"They bring awareness and that's what helps change to occur."

The sound of police sirens cut through our conversation. Her eyes darted towards the street that held the protest. "Shit, that's not good."

"I'm surprised you're not out there still."

She looked at me again. "It's not worth my while to leave this car. The protest organiser has enough people helping her today that she won't miss me."

"Why isn't it worth your while to leave?" I was fucking fascinated with her and wondered what shit she was into that made her follow Bronze's orders.

The back door of the car on my side opened, cutting off our conversation, and Bronze barked, "Out!"

She lifted a brow as she hit me with another smile. "When the cop says jump, it's time to fucking jump."

Before I could say anything, Bronze banged on the roof. "Come on, Devil, I don't have all fucking day."

"Aah, I see you know him, too," she murmured, her eyes dropping to my neck again.

"Yeah." I tried to move, tried to turn away from her to exit the car, but the pull was too great. She'd fucking captivated me. I could have sat and talked with her all day.

Pointing at my neck, she said, "That's Lawson's work, isn't it? I love his tats." Holding out one of her arms, she added, "This sleeve is all his."

Her arm was a fucking masterpiece. One I wouldn't have time to admire because Bronze yanked me out of the car right at that fucking moment.

"Fuck, Bronze," I complained as I stumbled. "I was in the middle of a fucking conversation."

He slammed the door shut behind me and reached for my hands. "Trust me when I tell you that you have nothing to say to that woman." He freed my hands and scowled at me. "I don't have time now to make sure you get on your bike and get out of here, but do King a favour and don't get caught up in anything here."

"What's going down with the club today? What shit aren't you telling me?"

He sucked in a deep breath. "Tell King to call me. Tell him I would have come to him this morning to warn him, but I didn't have time because of family shit."

"Jesus, that's it? That's all you're gonna give me?"

His jaw clenched. "Go. I've got stuff to do." With that, he stepped around me and got in his car.

I watched him drive away, wondering what the fuck was going down today. None of it sounded good.

***

"You're late." King cut his conversation with Hyde short to throw his accusation at me the minute I entered the clubhouse bar later that morning.

"Yeah, I got caught up in a fucking animal protest and Bronze of all people was there. He detained me in the back of his car for a while."

"You dropped that stuff off to Jen?"

"Yeah. She okay, King? I think she was vomiting before I got there, but when I asked her, she said she was fine." I omitted the part about her snapping at me when I told her she looked anything but fine and the part where she closed the door in my face when I suggested she let me in to help her.

He brushed it off. "She's okay." If he wasn't concerned, I wasn't going to waste my time worrying about her. Jen had a good dose of bitch in her, and over the course of the year I'd known her before she left King, I'd learnt to steer clear of her. I had no intentions of doing anything but that this time, too.

A quick glance around the bar told me the boys were gearing up for what we had planned at midday. We'd worked closely with Silver Hell over the past few months putting together plans to wipe out Gambarro. The first strike would take place that day.

"Devil, you're with me, today," Hyde said, taking a step away from King. The tense body language between the two of them told me everything I needed to know—things weren't good between our club president and VP.

Hyde had been late for Church yesterday, angering King. That anger remained, and I wondered when it would ease. Hyde's mood was worse than ever, and King's patience with him had disappeared.

I gave Hyde a nod. "Whatever you need."

Nitro and Kick entered the bar and made their way to us. One look at Nitro and I knew something was up. He eyed King. "Dragon's not answering his phone. I don't have a good feeling about this, King. You want us to head over to their clubhouse and check things out?"

Before King could answer, his phone rang. "What?" he barked when he answered it. Silence for a moment, and then—"Bring him in." Ending the call, he looked at us with a frown.

"There's a guy at the front gate who claims to be a fucking cop with info I need to hear about the Gambarro plans." Raking his fingers through his hair, he roared, "Fuck! This is the last fucking thing we need."

"Shit," I muttered. "Bronze said for you to call him and that he didn't have time to call you this morning because of family stuff he had going on. He knew something was going down."

"Christ." King scowled as he processed my words and then turned at the sound of men entering the clubhouse.

A moment later, Jacko stood in front of us with a guy who looked anything but a cop. Jerking his chin at the guy, Jacko said, "Says he's a fed. Showed me his badge, but I don't know if it's legit."

At first glance, I wouldn't have assumed the guy was a cop. Tattoos covered one of his arms, a scruffy beard filled half his face, and his clothes would have allowed him to fit in at any of the pubs we frequented. But when I looked closer and noticed his clean fingernails and expensive looking shoes that I'd never seen anyone I knew wear, I figured he could well be a pig.

He pulled out his badge and showed it to King. "Detective Ryland. I'm here to discuss your plans for Angelo Gambarro."

King inspected the badge. "What plans?"

Ryland shoved his badge in his pocket. "The plans you've been making with Silver Hell to take down Gambarro's organisation and kill him. The plans you are going to walk away from in order to avoid me investigating your club and generally making your life hell."

King's jaw clenched and his shoulders squared. "I don't know how the hell you know this shit, but I'm going to make it my mission to find out."

Ryland had some fucking balls. He stepped closer to King, invading his space, and pushed his face towards Kings. "You're going to leave it be, King. I'm not a man you want to fuck with. We've been watching you and your boys for some time now, and the shit we know about Storm would be enough to put you away for a long fucking time." He cocked his head. "But maybe you want to spend time with Ghost. How long's it been since you've seen him?"

King's whole body tensed and his face contorted with anger. "Leave him the fuck out of it."

"Yeah, ten years behind bars for your club is enough to fuck with a man, so I'm guessing you and Ghost aren't on good terms these days."

"You've got no fucking idea what you're talking about," King spat. "And as far as putting any of my men behind bars, I'd like to see you prove a fucking thing in court. You're full of shit. Nothing we do is traceable and we sure as fuck don't leave evidence behind that you motherfuckers can use against us."

Ryland stepped away from King. "You go near Gambarro and we'll test that theory. But hear me when I say that we do have proof and we won't hesitate to use it." He took a few steps towards the door before pausing. "Also know that we're watching you 24/7 at the moment. There's no way for you to do anything without us knowing about it." With that, he exited the room. Jacko followed him to ensure he left the property.

King slammed his hand down on the bar. "Motherfucker!" Turning to Hyde, he ordered, "Call Dragon and see if they've had a visit from the feds, too. I'm calling Bronze."

Hyde nodded and pulled his phone out as he walked away in search of a quiet place to make the call. King did the same, heading to a corner of the bar. I watched as his face and body language changed during the call. Whatever Bronze told him, angered him more than Ryland had.

When he came back to where I stood with Nitro and Kick, he said, "The cops have a guy undercover with Silver Hell. That's how they know our shit. It seems that Gambarro is tied up with some counterfeiting operation and the feds are watching him to figure out who else is involved and who is running it. We kill him, they lose the one person they have who can lead them to more information."

Hyde joined us. "Dragon had the same visit we did. That's why he wasn't answering his phone this morning."

"What's his plan now?" Nitro asked.

"Says he can't afford to piss the feds off, so he's backing away from Gambarro for the moment. He did say, though, that he wants to move forward in the future, once this all dies down," Hyde said.

King turned silent, weighing up options by the look on his face. We all knew to stay silent while he thought it through. Finally, he said, "Gambarro goes on hold, but we keep eyes on him. Hyde, you and Kick stay on top of that and report back daily." Eyeing Nitro, he said, "You and Devil pay a visit to Ghost. I want to know if the cops have anything there."

Nitro frowned. "Ghost wouldn't talk."

King scowled. "Ghost is capable of anything, Nitro. Find out what we need to know."

I'd never met Ghost, but I'd heard the stories about him and King. No love was lost there. Not after Ghost made a play for King's woman years ago.

Nitro didn't seem convinced, but he nodded. "Will do."

As I followed him outside, I said, "On a scale of one to ten, how bad is this likely to get if Ghost is involved?"

He slowed so he could meet my gaze. "I'd say an eleven."

Chapter Two

Hailee

"You nail that chick last night?"

I glanced up from my phone and eyed my bandmate Hollis, who'd just asked one of my other bandmates that question. "Am I invisible?" I'd told him enough times lately to stop discussing the groupies they banged while I was in the room, yet, he continued to do it.

"Fuck, Hailee, this is how we've always talked. Even with you in the room," he muttered. Gesturing at our other bandmates, he said, "Back me up, fuckers."

Before either Dylan or Trent could say anything, I stood and said, "I know, but I'm over it. I don't care that you do it, but I'd just rather you talk about your groupies when I'm not around." Grabbing my bag, I said, "I'm gonna go grab a drink before our set." The need to get out of this room was intense. My usually easy-going mood had disappeared, replaced with irritation I couldn't shake. And I knew it wasn't the guys causing it, but they were the ones who'd cop it if I didn't leave.

Dylan frowned. "We haven't finalised our set list yet."

"Let's just go with the same as last night." I didn't wait for anyone's reply before exiting the room and heading towards the bar.

God knew, I needed a drink. It'd been a long day with the animal protest and then work. An argument with my grandmother right before coming to the pub had put me on edge. We hardly ever argued, but when we did, I usually realised she was right. And fuck it, I didn't want her to be right this time.

"You look like you could murder someone," Doug said as I leaned on the counter of the bar. He was my favourite Fling bartender, and Fling was my favourite pub. All of this caused me to smile for the first time in at least two hours.

Sighing, I said, "Yeah, myself."

He placed a drink on the counter and slid it my way. "Saw you coming. Knew you needed this just by looking at you."

I glanced down at the French Martini he'd made me and then smiled up at him. Before I lifted it to my mouth, I said, "You're an absolute star, Mr Gilbert."

He grinned the sexy grin that nearly caused me to sleep with him once ages ago. I'd come to my senses when I'd realised I didn't want to chance ruining the awesome friendship we had. "And yet, she still refuses to sleep with me."

My smile morphed into a grin to match his. "And yet, he doesn't care as much as he makes out he does, because he knows we're better off as friends."

"I hope Wayne knows how lucky he is, Hailee."

My smile disappeared and my shoulders slumped a little. Placing my cocktail down, I said, "What do you really think of Wayne?"

Many of our conversations revolved around my dating life. After a shitty relationship of mine ended two years ago, I'd spent the time since then trying to find love. Without much success. I'd been dating Wayne for almost a month, and I thought he was a great guy—thoughtful, stable, steady job, seemed settled in life—but my grandmother had told me that afternoon that he wasn't the one for me. She said she saw no fire between the two of us.

"You want the truth, babe? Or aren't you ready for that yet?" Doug's eyes held mine while he waited for my reply. There was so much kindness there that I knew he'd give it to me gently. And he'd only ever tell me the God's honest truth as he saw it.

I nodded. "Give it to me."

He rested his arms on the counter. "Wayne's a good guy, no doubt about it, but I don't see any chemistry between the two of you. He doesn't light you up, and I don't think he's made you any happier than you already were." He leaned towards me. "Hailee, when you're with the right man, he'll make you smile more than you ever have. You'll feel more than you ever have. Hell, you might even argue more than you ever have with a guy. The point is, there'll be passion. I don't see that with Wayne."

"Have you been talking to my grandmother? She told me today that there's no fire between the two of us."

He grinned again as he straightened. "Always did love Jean. That woman knows her shit. She coming to watch you sing tonight?"

"No, it's Monday." At his frown, I added, "Monday nights are reserved for *Law and Order* reruns."

Doug's attention shifted for a moment as he looked past me. Lifting his chin, he spoke to someone standing behind me. "Hey, man, the usual?"

"Yeah." The guy's deep voice filtered through the air as he moved to stand next to me.

"Tatum here tonight?" Doug asked as he poured two beers.

I turned to look up at the guy. Jesus, he was built. And hot. I had to work hard to keep my tongue in my mouth.

He shook his head. "Not yet, but she's on her way."

"Billy got her working hard?"

The guy's jaw clenched, and I got the distinct impression from the way his lips pressed together that whoever Billy was, this man didn't much like him. "When doesn't he?"

Doug nodded. "Yeah, it seems that way lately. She hasn't been here as much, that's for sure."

A redheaded woman interrupted us. "Nitro, where's Tatum? I thought she'd be here by now."

"I thought she was coming with you."

"Nope, she rang to say she'd meet me here, and because I'm late, I assumed she'd be here already." She checked her watch. "Fuck, Billy must have dumped more work on her. I swear I'm gonna have words with that man. It's not fair how much shit he's got her doing these days."

Nitro took the drinks Doug passed him. "Yeah, well if he doesn't pull his head in soon, *I'll* be having words with him. And I don't give a fuck if Tatum doesn't like what I have to say."

"Oh, fuck," the woman muttered as Nitro left. Her eyes met Doug's. "The last thing any of us need is Nitro having words with Billy."

"I can't imagine anyone wanting to have words with Nitro," Doug said. "You want your usual, Monroe?"

Before I could stop it, my mouth opened and out gushed, "Oh, I love that name!"

Monroe's gaze met mine and she smiled, and when she smiled, she radiated the kind of warmth anyone would want to be next to. Her whole face lit up and I couldn't help but be drawn to the beauty she wore like a second skin. She was all gorgeous curves, stunning long red hair, flawless skin made up perfectly, and sparkling eyes. If I was the kind of woman to feel jealousy, I'd feel it with this woman.

"Thank you, honey," she said. "What's your name?"

"Hailee."

"I love that, too." Her gaze zeroed in on my cocktail when I drank some more of it. "Oooh, what is that? I need one of those." She looked up at Doug. "You've been holding out on me."

He chuckled. "Babe, I haven't been holding out. You've just been set on drinking Jägerbombs lately."

She pouted, her red lipstick catching my eye. I wondered if she was a make-up artist. Or maybe a hairdresser. Both her hair and make-up were amazing, so I figured she could be either. Clicking her fingers at him, she said, "Start me off with a Jägerbomb and then make me whatever that cocktail is." She settled on a stool next to me as she issued her request.

He arched a brow and she added, "Please," with a grin. Then—"Wait,"—glancing at me, she asked, "Do you want a Jäger with me?"

"Sure, I could do with one tonight. Or two."

Her grin spread further across her face. "Awesome. Two please, Doug."

My phone sounded with a text as he started on our drinks.

Dylan: You good?

Me: I will be.

Dylan: You reckon that'll kick in tonight? Or should I warn the guys to strap on some armour?

Me: You a funny guy *said in best foreign accent*

Dylan: Just looking out for my girl.

Me: Love you, D. Now leave me be. I'm getting wasted.

Dylan: Jesus. We've got music to play. Hold off on the turps.

Me: Just fucking with you. I'm only having two drinks.

Dylan: Famous last fucking words. I'm coming now.

"Girl, you are smiling like a loon," Monroe said. Lifting her chin at my phone, she added, "That your man?"

I placed my phone on the counter and reached for one of the drinks Doug had made us. "No, it's my bandmate."

"You two aren't together?"

"No. He's one of my closest friends." *Now that Tricia was gone.* I lifted my Jägerbomb up. "Cheers."

We threw the drinks down our throats and I remembered why I didn't drink Jäger often.

"You don't love it so much?" Monroe asked as she took in the face I pulled.

"It's not my favourite, no." I caught Doug's eye and raised my empty Martini glass while indicating that I'd like another.

She laughed. "We need to drink together more often. You just need to drink more of it and then you'll start to like it."

"Oh, God, is my cousin trying to make you drink Jäger?"

I turned to find a blonde woman standing behind us, a look of amusement on her face.

Monroe turned also. "Oh, hush, Tatum. I need to find at least one person who wants to drink it with me."

Tatum was gorgeous, but in a completely different way to her cousin. Where Monroe was ample curves, Tatum was slender; where Monroe was mostly clean skin, Tatum was inked all over; and where Monroe's eyes held warmth, Tatum's held hesitation.

Her eyes met mine, narrowing. "Have we met before?"

"I don't think so."

"You're so familiar to me."

Monroe's face washed over with recognition. "I've been sitting here thinking the same thing, and I've just figured it out. You're the singer in Cherry Vivid, aren't you? The band that plays here a couple of times most weeks."

"Yes, that's me." I'd never seen them here before, but that didn't mean much, because usually I was either working the stage or dancing. I didn't spend a lot of time socialising unless you counted the time I spent with my bandmates or with Doug.

"Tatum!" A guy's voice cut through the air, and a sense of having heard that voice hit me.

Tatum turned at the same time I looked past her at the man walking our way. My tummy did flips like it was a freaking Olympic gymnast, and my legs threatened to give way when I saw who the deep rumble belonged to.

The guy I'd met in the back of Aaron's car that morning.

Devil.

Everything about him was sexy, from his chiselled jaw, to his muscular arms, to the scruff on his face, to the ink that covered his skin, to the way he sauntered my way with a knowing expression on his face. It was the kind of expression that told me he wasn't a man who hid his attraction to a woman, but I should have remembered that from when I'd met him earlier. He sure hadn't hidden it then. He'd looked at me like he wanted to devour me. Pretty much the same way he looked at me now.

Blue eyes met mine as he came closer, and his lips curled up into a smile that could wipe all thoughts from a woman's mind. *All thoughts except those about him.* "It's my animal protest girl." The way he said *my* only caused more Olympic-worthy somersaults in my belly.

"And it's my protector," I bantered back, wanting him to never stop talking. Guilty thoughts about Wayne swam through my mind for at least a moment, and I did my best to turn them off. *We aren't serious. We've made no commitments to each other. He said just the other day that it was a bit of fun to see where it went. Surely it's okay to flirt with another guy while we're seeing...*

"You two know each other?" Tatum asked.

Devil's eyes held mine. "No, I don't even know her name."

"Hailee," I said, not letting his eyes go either.

"Hailee," he murmured, my name sliding through his lips so damn huskily that I wanted to ask him to say it again. *And again.*

"And you're Devil?" It was what Aaron had called him that morning, but it seemed more like a nickname than a real name.

He took a step closer to me. "Yeah, Devil."

My breathing sped up a little at his proximity. "That's a nickname, right?"

His smile never left his face. "It is."

"You're not going to tell me your real name?"

"Nope."

"Let me guess, only the special girls get that."

"Every girl's special, darlin', but none of them get that."

"Oh, you're smooth. What about the story behind the nickname? Will you give me that?"

He leant his face closer. "If I tell you that, will you have a drink with me?"

"I can't. I've got work to do, and—"

Dylan joined us and cut me off. "And if she has another drink, she won't be able to sing tonight." He moved so he stood next to me. Right next to me, with his arm draped over my shoulder. His way of telling a guy to back the fuck off.

I sighed. Dylan and I had gone head-to-head numerous times over his protective ways, but he refused to stop. Just like my damn brother.

Devil seemed surprised. "Sing?"

Monroe chimed in. "Hailee's the singer in Cherry Vivid." At Devil's frown, she added, "The band that plays here all the time."

"I haven't had the pleasure of watching you perform yet," he said.

I hit him with a sexy smile. "Well, you'll get to tonight if you stick around."

"I think I just might, darlin'."

Our attention to each other was diverted by those around us then. Tatum pulled him aside to discuss something while Dylan dragged me back to the band so we could finalise our song choices for that night. The butterflies in my belly didn't ease, though. Devil had stirred them up in a way they hadn't been awakened in years.

Chapter Three

Devil

I sucked back some beer as I watched Hailee sing a Pink song. Jesus, she could belt out a tune. The band had been playing for a good twenty minutes, and I hadn't been able to take my eyes off her. Between her voice, the way she interacted with the audience and her beauty, she fucking owned the stage.

Tatum shifted her face closer to mine to say, "Your girl's good."

I chuckled. "*My* girl?"

Her eyes met mine and she smiled. "You'll make her yours for at least a night. It's what you do."

Lifting a brow, I queried her, "It's what I do? Where the fuck do you get that idea from?"

"You forget I'm a lawyer, Devil. I see everything, and I've seen you around. You're a lover, not a fighter, right?"

I drank some more beer and nodded. "True, I am. But you make me sound like an asshole who fucks women for one night and doesn't look back."

"I'm not saying it's a bad thing. I'm just stating facts."

"Okay, so maybe I have had some casual sex lately, but that's only because there didn't end up being any connection with those chicks afterwards." Fuck knew why it was so important to me that Tatum not think I was an asshole, but it was. I'd gotten to know her well over the last few months and respected her enough to care what she thought of me.

"No connection? As in, no attraction besides sex?"

"Yeah, nothing that made me want to dedicate time, you know?" I drained my bottle of beer and placed it on the table we sat at with Nitro and Monroe. "I don't know, I need a spark, some passion... or some shit, and I'm just not feeling it with anyone lately."

Nitro cut in. "When you're finished with your relationship counselling, you and I need to discuss tomorrow."

Tatum ran her fingers through Nitro's hair. "You okay?"

He leant his elbows on his knees and took a moment before answering. Glancing sideways at her, he shook his head. "Lot of shit going on, Vegas. I've got a headache from hell."

"You wanna go home?"

He sat up again and laid his arm across the back of her chair. "No, we'll stay for a while."

Nitro had come a long fucking way since he'd met Tatum. He and I'd had a shitty day and I knew he didn't want to be here tonight, yet he stayed for Tatum. A long fucking way.

Tatum finished her drink and stood, reaching for Nitro. "Come on, champ, take me home."

His lips twitched, a smile almost forming. Standing, he slid an arm around her waist and pulled her close. He whispered something in her ear before looking at me. "I'll come by your place at eight tomorrow morning. We're gonna see Ghost if it fucking kills us."

We'd spent hours this afternoon attempting a visit with Ghost, but there'd been some issue at the prison and we hadn't been granted a visit. Nitro had asked Tatum to help, and she'd come through with the goods after talking with some of her legal buddies.

Tatum turned to Monroe. "You want a lift home, babe?"

"Yeah, thanks." Eyes on me as she stood, she said, "Good luck with Hailee."

I glanced at Hailee on the stage. "I never need luck, Monroe."

"I bet."

Nitro met my gaze. "Be ready for tomorrow, brother. Ghost can be a motherfucker when he wants to be."

Yeah, I'd heard those stories, too. I lifted my chin. "Go home. I'll see you tomorrow."

After they'd left, I made my way back to the bar and ordered another beer. "How much longer is the band on for?" I asked Doug as he handed it over.

"Don't fuck with her, Devil," he said, pissing me off.

"What the fuck does that mean?" I'd been coming to this pub for years, and as far as I was aware, Doug and I were on good terms. This attitude off him wasn't fucking appreciated.

"It means that Hailee means something to me and I won't stand by and watch you use her."

"Jesus, does everyone think I'm an asshole when it comes to women?"

"Your history speaks for itself. I can't remember the last time you dated a woman."

I took a long slug of my beer. "It was two years ago, asshole, and *she* left me, not the other way around. And that was after two years of living together. I'm not a complete fucking bastard."

He leant on the counter. "I'm not saying you're a bastard, and I have nothing against you sleeping with whoever you want. Just don't fuck with Hailee. That's all I'm saying."

I was ready to tell him to go fuck himself when Hailee's voice cut through the crowd, announcing they were taking a half-hour break. Without another word to Doug, I headed towards the stage.

Hailee met me halfway, her eyes roaming appreciatively over my body before finding my gaze. A slow smile hit her lips. "You're still here."

I returned her smile. "You think a man could walk away while you're singing? Besides, I owe you a drink."

"I never said yes to a drink."

"That word may not have left your mouth, but it sure as fuck was written all over your body, darlin'." I tipped my bottle of beer to my lips and waited for her reply. This conversation could last hours and lead nowhere, and I wouldn't give a shit. I just wanted to be in her presence and soak her sexiness into my bones.

She moved into my personal space, our bodies almost touching. "I've got lots of words written all over my body, but yes isn't one of them."

I closed the tiny distance between us and traced a finger over her lips. She didn't stop me—a fair indication that she was as keen for this as I was. "How about I buy you a drink and we start figuring out how you'd like me to get you from clothed to naked."

"We could have a drink, but getting me naked could take some time."

I grinned. "I'm all about the challenge."

"Yeah, maybe not this one."

Fuck, when I finally got her under me, it was going to be fireworks. I ran my finger down her face, neck, and down to her collarbone. My eyes dropped to the tight, sleeveless black top she had on. The one that revealed a cleavage I'd like to get between. When I found her eyes again, I said, "I've never walked away from a challenge in my life, darlin'. I'm not about to now."

She gripped my hand when I started trailing my finger over her skin, down to her tits. Halting my progress, like I had hoped she would, because a yes given too soon was nowhere near as fun as a no dragged out, she said, "I'm not single."

"How *not single* are you? Like, are we talking close-to-marriage single or he's-barely-gotten-his-dick-wet single?" I'd never cut in on a serious relationship, but she wasn't giving me those kinds of vibes.

She didn't skip a beat. "Let's just say his dick is almost dry, but let's also say that I'm not looking for an alternative at this point."

"Let's also call it bullshit. I haven't met a woman more open to an alternative in a long fucking time." I dipped my face so my mouth was next to her ear. "We both know that if I pursued the fuck out of you tonight, you'd be bending that sweet ass over and letting me fuck you any way I wanted."

Again, she didn't stumble, and gave it back to me just as good. "I think we both know that me bending over for you is a long way off. As for letting you fuck me any way you want... that would be after you prove you know your way around a pussy."

"I know my way around a pussy better than I know my way around my dick. And that's saying something because—"

She silenced me by placing her finger against my lips. I loved her skin on mine and had to restrain myself from forcing her to keep it there. "Let me guess, your dick gets a good workout?"

Fuck.

This woman was fucking made for me, and it was taking every ounce of strength I had not to put my hands all over her body. "A French Martini, right?"

Her forehead wrinkled in confusion. "Huh?"

"That's what you're drinking tonight, right?"

"It is. How did you—"

I cut her off and dipped my mouth to her ear again. "I'm the kind of man who always makes it a point to know things, Hailee. I'm also the kind of man who doesn't give up, so let me buy you a drink and spend some time with you."

I saw the moment she gave in when I pulled my face away from hers. Unfortunately, it was also the moment her boyfriend decided to show his face.

"Hey, babe," he said as he quickly kissed her cheek. *Her fucking cheek.* If Hailee was mine, no fucking way would I greet her with a kiss on her cheek. Especially not if she was talking with another guy. I'd be making it really fucking clear to him that she was mine and that he should back the fuck off and never go near her again.

She turned into him, but I caught the hesitation. His arm slid around her waist, but his attention wasn't on her. And it wasn't on me, either, which it should have been. His gaze had wandered to something behind me, while Hailee's eyes still held mine.

"Thanks for watching us play tonight," she said, letting me know this conversation was done.

"I'll be back to see more soon."

I watched them walk away, my attention on her ass and my mind stuck on what made her tick. She wanted what I wanted. I just had to figure out what was holding her back.

***

Ghost sat down across from Nitro and me at the prison the next day, and with one look at him, I knew this was going to be a hard conversation. And probably not one that would get us anywhere.

He glared at Nitro. "King sent you to do his dirty work?"

Nitro clenched his jaw. "How are you, brother?"

Ghost raised a brow. "Are you asking because you genuinely care, or is it the kind of question you ask to break the ice before you try to fuck a man in the ass?"

Nitro shoved his fingers through his hair and then rested his elbows on the table separating us from Ghost. "When the fuck have I ever tried to screw you over, Ghost?"

Ghost continued to glare at him while we all sat in silence. Finally he blew out a long breath. "Always a first time for everything, especially when the feds are breathing down the club's neck."

"So you know about that?" Nitro asked.

"Yeah, they came to see me a couple of weeks ago."

"And?"

Ghost didn't answer him but rather, glanced at me. "Who are you?"

Nitro cut in. "It doesn't matter who the fuck he is, answer my question."

The dark eyes I was staring into flared with anger, and again he said, "Who are you?"

"Devil," I answered.

"You been a member for long?"

"Seven years."

He leant back in his seat, stretching his legs out in front of him, his arms crossed over his chest. To anyone not part of this conversation, he would have looked casual, but I saw the tension that had settled in him. "So you joined a few years after they fucked me over."

"Fuck," Nitro bit out. "No one fucked you over, Ghost. When are you gonna let that shit go?"

Ghost's anger came to life and he pushed out of his chair, slamming his fist on the table. "When are you gonna see King for the motherfucker he is, Nitro? He's had you on that fucking leash for years, ready to do his dirty work whenever he says so."

Nitro shot out of his seat, a matching look of fury on his face. Before he could lose his shit, though, I stood too and placed my hand against his chest. Pushing him back, I cautioned, "Brother, this isn't the time. Sit down and let's get what we came for before the guards kick us out."

His lips pressed together and his eyes cut to mine. After a few deep breaths, he nodded and stepped down.

I turned to Ghost. "Sit the fuck down. You need to hear what we have to say."

He stood his ground. "I don't need to do jack."

"Yeah, you do," Nitro said. "For Ashlyn's sake."

Whoever Ashlyn was, she meant something to Ghost, because his face clouded over with menace. "You fucking touch her and I swear to fucking God you'll live to regret that decision."

"You give us what we need and I won't go near her. The decision is in your hands."

"Motherfucker," Ghost muttered before dragging the seat back to the table and sitting. "I fucking gave Storm everything and this is the way you repay me."

Nitro and I sat. He shook his head. "No, we looked after you, but you chose to walk away and be a cunt about it all."

"What would you have done, Nitro, if you'd been in my shoes? King stripped my vice presidency from me because I made one fucking mistake, and then he did everything in his power to cut me from the club. He chose pussy over a brother. Tell me that you wouldn't have taken that as a reason to walk away."

I was confused, not knowing the full story, but I was under the impression that Ghost was still a club member. "You left the club?"

Ghost met my gaze. "I'm nomad now. Stuck in a fucking prison for the shit I did for a club that didn't have my back after all."

"For fuck's sake, Ghost, when did you start making shit up in your head?" Nitro glanced at me. "He made a play for King's woman—"

Ghost cut in. "When I was fucking drunk!"

"So that makes it okay?" Nitro threw out.

Ghost raked his fingers through his hair. "It was a bad move, but you can't tell me you haven't done dumb shit after a few drinks."

Nitro leant forward. "But it wasn't the first time, was it, Ghost? You'd done that shit before. King forced Jen to tell him the truth after you were locked up. Turned out you hit on her almost every time you got wasted, and she didn't tell King because she didn't want to cause problems in the club."

"Yeah, well that didn't give King the right to take my vice presidency away and give it to Hyde." He looked at me. "Does he still put pussy before his brothers?"

I'd heard just about enough. "I've never seen King choose a woman over his brothers. And I'm betting there's more to this story than the shit you're spinning."

"There sure fucking is," Nitro said, but didn't elaborate.

Ghost didn't respond. He simply sat there seething.

"How about we get down to business?" I suggested, having had enough of this conversation. Ghost didn't appear to be the kind of person to ever consider he could be wrong. "What did the feds want when they spoke with you?"

Ghost crossed his arms over his chest again. He sat in silence for a beat, but quickly came to his senses. "They were asking questions about Storm's drug trade."

Nitro frowned. "What, from ten years ago when you actually had something to do with it?"

"Yeah, that and they also wanted to know what I knew about the shit that went down with Moses."

Fuck. This couldn't be good. The Moses incident should never have seen the light of day. We'd buried that, never to be heard of again.

The vein in Nitro's temple pulsed. "What the fuck do they know about Moses?"

"I don't know. I told them I knew nothing."

"So they just left it at that?"

"For now. I've a feeling they'll be back, though."

"Why?" I demanded.

Smug delight flashed on his face. "Because they want to bring King down."

The vein that had pulsed at Nitro's temple damn near pushed through his skin. "And let me guess, you want to help with that. Except, if you do, all bets are off the table as far as Ashlyn's concerned." He stood. "Are we on the same page?"

"Yeah, we're on the same fucking page, Nitro," Ghost replied. "But when I get out of here, you'd better watch your back, motherfucker. No one threatens my sister and gets away with it."

"You think you're getting out of here?" Nitro took a step away from the table. "You might wanna stop making threats if you ever want that to happen."

I wasn't sure what to make of Ghost and his threats, but Nitro's? I'd never cross him. If he threatened to find a way to keep me in jail, I'd believe every word he said.

As Nitro left the table, I said to Ghost, "Not sure how well you know him, but I'd never fuck with Nitro. Make sure you call us when you hear from the feds again."

Chapter Four

Hailee

"I need your hands on me, Hails. Tell me what I've gotta do for you to stop saying no to me," Dylan said, a look of defeat on his face.

I flopped down onto his couch next to him and reached for the beer in his hand. After I took a sip, I said, "Dude, I've been working these hands and arms all day and I'm exhausted. Maybe if you actually book an appointment with me while I'm at work, you'd have more luck."

I was sympathetic to his cause—Dylan spent his days laying bricks to make ends meet—but eight-hour-plus shifts massaging people exhausted me.

He grabbed his beer back. "I can't afford an appointment with you. Your boss charges way too much for massages."

"That's only because you're a tight-ass. I mean, the amount of money you spend on beer could fund a couple of massages a week."

"Are you two arguing over fucking massages again?"

I glanced up at our bandmate Trent as he entered the living room and sat on the end of the couch. "Aren't we always?"

He grinned and threw me a wink. "Yeah, at least Dylan's consistent with his shit. You always know what you're gonna get with him."

After close to two years playing with these guys, I knew them inside out, and Trent was right—Dylan was consistent in his hounding me for free massages. Just like Trent was consistent with harassing me to help him with his girlfriend dilemmas.

"How's Pam going? Have you managed to break up with her yet?" I asked him. He'd been dating her for three weeks and had been complaining about her for almost as long.

He grimaced. "Fuck, I can hardly get a word in with her, Hails."

"So that would be a no, then? You pussied out again?" He was way too nice and always trying to extricate himself from relationships he didn't want to be in.

"Who was that guy you were talking to last night before Wayne got there? Looked like he was all over you," Trent said.

"You trying to change the subject?" I asked.

He grinned. It was the grin that always got him out of trouble. Not that he was in trouble now, but it was his way of telling me he didn't want to continue the conversation about Pam. "You know me too well."

I decided to let him off the hook this once. Hell, who was I kidding? Trent was always being let off the hook in one way or another. Everyone loved the guy—enough to let him avoid dealing with whatever problem he'd found himself in. "The guy's name is Devil, but other than that, I don't know who he is."

"Gotta say, I was surprised Wayne didn't take a shot at him," Dylan said.

Wayne never would.

And that told me everything I needed to know about my relationship with Wayne. It wasn't that I wanted him to have a go at another man who gave me attention, but I wanted him to at least feel something about it. *Anything*. Even if he just made a casual remark about it. I wanted him to acknowledge it in some way. We'd been getting closer over the last few weeks, and I had been looking for a sign from him as to whether the relationship might develop into something more permanent. He could have used Devil's flirting with me as a way to stake his claim, because even though he hadn't heard our conversation, he had to have seen Devil lean into me while he spoke into my ear. The fact that didn't bother him bothered me.

But, the thing about Wayne was that he was safe. He was a good guy, and after the shit I'd been through with my last relationship, all I wanted was a good guy who I could trust to do the right thing by me.

"You see yourself with him for the long haul?" Trent asked.

I pushed up off the couch. I didn't want to talk about Wayne anymore. Looking down at them both, I said, "Are we gonna practise, or not?"

Trent lifted a brow as he stood. "Look who's changing the subject now."

I poked my tongue at him. Continuing to change the subject, I said, "Anyone hear from Hollis today? Are we thinking he's gonna make it tonight?" Hollis had a record of missing band practice, and tonight was a night I didn't want him to miss. We had new songs to practise.

"He texted me about an hour ago," Dylan said as we made our way out to his garage for practice. "He should be here in the next half hour. His boss was making him stay late today."

Hollis was an accountant, which had surprised me when I'd first met him two years ago. I'd put the call out for musicians to form a band with me, and he'd turned up straight from work in his tie, looking way too respectable to be a drummer. However, the minute he got behind his drum kit and ripped his tie off, he'd blown me away with his talent. These days I never saw the tie. Not even when he was wearing it. All I saw was the dirty-as-fuck drummer who could drink all of us under the table while lining women up to screw. Definitely not too respectable to be a drummer.

"Okay, let's run through these songs," I said. "Hollis knows them like the back of his hand, so it'll be good for us to go through them before he gets here, and then he can just jump in." While he was a dirty guy always looking for his next lay, Hollis surprised me with his ability to tap into his emotions when it came to writing songs. His lyrics were full of deep thoughts and often about love. He wrote most of our band's music. I helped when he needed it, and sometimes I came up with new material for him to work into a song.

Dylan picked up his guitar. "I forgot to tell you guys that I booked us for a wedding next Saturday."

Dylan took care of all our bookings and often forgot to tell us about a gig until the week it was on. I glanced at him. "I'll make you a deal. You start using that online calendar I showed you last week and log our gigs as soon as you get them, and I'll start considering giving you a massage every now and then."

As he began strumming his guitar, he smirked and said, "Come on, Hails, you gotta put out if you want the goods. None of this *considering* business. For every gig I schedule in your online thing, I want a massage from you."

God, the shit you had to do to get a man to do the shit he was supposed to do. But at least we might finally know our dates in advance. "You're on."

Trent started playing his guitar and I grabbed the mic. It was time to lose ourselves in the beats and drown out everything else in our heads.

***

"Hailee, are you even listening to me?" Leona asked over lunch in the park the next day. She swept away the few strands of her long blonde hair that had stuck to her face as the wind whipped through the air. The weather was bipolar that day; the morning had kicked off with promised heat, but the wind had slowly crept in, and the forecast was for a storm later.

I'd just finished eating my sandwich and had leant back, resting on my elbows on the grass, but I sat up straight as I answered her. "Kind of, but I'm watching that man over there"—I pointed at the guy in my sights—"because he just kicked his dog."

Leona and I had worked together for two years and we'd become good friends, so she knew how much I loathed people who hurt animals. "You want me to come with you while you tell him off?"

"You sure?" The last time she'd helped me out, or should I say, the last time I *dragged* her with me to a protest, she'd been knocked to the ground and broke her wrist.

She pffted and said, "Of course. I'm your ninja warrior sidekick"—she waved her hand in the air—"or some shit like that." Scrambling to her feet, she added, "Besides, when do I ever get some fun in my life? Jerry has me under lock and key and wrapped in cotton wool when I'm with him. I need you to lead me astray."

I groaned as I stood. "Jesus, that man of yours must hate you spending time with me." Some of the situations I'd gotten us in over the years ran through my mind—the time we'd been locked up for half a day, the time we'd managed to cause a brawl in a bar when I'd accidentally pissed a guy off and another one had stood up for me, and not to mention the time we had a minor car accident in her car because I'd distracted her by drawing her attention to a group of hot guys walking down the street. Jerry had almost lost his shit with me over that car accident, but being the good friend she was, Leona had placated him with promises of hot sex. Mind you, Jerry's idea of hot sex and my idea of hot sex were two very different things. I loved Jerry for the good man he was, but no way could I have ever married him. I would have been bored within a week.

"He doesn't hate you. He just wishes we'd do stuff like... I don't know, quiet stuff."

I burst out laughing. "You mean like sitting home on a Saturday night knitting and discussing our menu plan for the next week? That kind of shit?"

She grinned. "Probably that kind of shit."

My gaze zeroed in on a woman who'd just approached the guy with the dog. She spoke quite angrily and snatched the dog leash from him. I expected him to retaliate, but he didn't. Instead, he turned and stalked out of the park.

I turned to Leona. "Looks like Jerry is saved from potential stress today." Reaching for my bag on the ground, I added, "We should probably get back to work. Rachel's looking for any opportunity to give me a warning these days." My boss had turned into a raging bitch from hell when her hubby left her for another woman two months ago, and since then my life at work had become a little nightmarish in so far as I never knew what to expect each day. Her moods swung swiftly from happy to fucked off with the world, and I just had to keep on my toes and do my best to stay off her radar.

"Oh God, same! And we've got IVF coming up again soon, so we need my pay cheque. I swear, if that bitch fires me, she won't know what hit her." Leona may have been one of the nicest people I knew, but even I knew she had a darker side. A "do not fucking cross me" side. I guessed, though, that three unsuccessful years of IVF would be enough to cause any woman to threaten those who crossed her when it came to having a baby.

"Is there anything I can do to help you guys?" It felt like a dumb question, because short of offering up my body to carry a child for them, there wasn't anything I could do. But the fixer in me needed to ask.

"Can you send a prayer up to the big fella and ask him to please just let me have one kid. Only one. I'm not greedy. Not anymore." The sadness I felt in her words sliced through my heart. Kids were all Leona and Jerry talked about. They'd been married for five years and had been planning a large family from the beginning. But these days, she would do anything just to have one child.

I reached for her hand and gave it a squeeze. "I can't remember the last time I prayed, but I'm gonna send one out for you guys tonight."

She squeezed my hand back and gave me a smile. "Thank you," she said softly, all her fire over Rachel gone. In its place were all the emotions tied to her pain. *God, I hope this round works for her.*

Having children wasn't something I spent a great deal of time thinking about. At this point in my life, getting through the day was sometimes all I could focus on. I'd been on a path two years ago, a path that I thought led somewhere I wanted to go. I'd quickly learnt that the very thing we wished for could turn on us at any moment and bring us crashing down into our own personal form of hell. Getting back on my feet after roaming through that hell had taken time, and most days I still felt like I was learning how to walk again. So thinking past where I was now, into a future that could possibly have children in it wasn't something I did often.

Chapter Five

Devil

"You take the back, I'm in the front," King said to me mid-morning on Friday. We stood outside a run-down old house in Blacktown, with grass almost up to our knees. The paint peeling on the house, the lack of lawn maintenance and the hole in the front door led me to believe no one lived there, but King was convinced the person he was looking for would be inside—the guy that had beaten up Jen.

"Sure," I said.

As I turned to slip around the side of the house, he grabbed hold of my shirt and halted me. When I glanced back at him, the angry glint I saw there caused me to stiffen. "You taking this seriously, Devil?" His words were too controlled. Hell, King was far too contained. Calm almost. But that was King when he was in the midst of his crazy.

Right before he was about to explode.

The eye of the storm.

"Yeah." I hadn't been, though. King had been on a mission all week to find this guy. He'd been in a kind of frenzy, and no one had been able to talk sense into him. Hyde had suggested he slow his shit down and think things through rather than being like a bull at a gate. King had only increased his maniacal efforts after that.

He stepped closer to me, so close I could hear his breathing. "You think I'm going overboard on this, too?"

I'd always been honest with him and wouldn't stop that now. Even if it earned me his displeasure. "What I'm trying to figure out is why you're going to such extremes, King? All this for a woman who screwed you over years ago?"

His crazy eyes stared into mine for what felt like minutes. Being under this intense scrutiny from him, though, was the norm, so I was used to it. If there was one thing King drilled into all club members, it was to be able to withstand an interrogation. He did it often enough for us to quickly work out how to hold up under those circumstances. King trusted no one and was all about being prepared for the potential threats that surrounded us. If the cops dragged a member in for questioning, he wanted them to be ready for it, and he'd done a good job prepping us. Each time someone had been interrogated, they'd withstood the cops' questions and kept the club safe.

Finally, he said, "I respect the fuck out of you, Devil, but you don't know mine and Jen's story. No one does. She may have screwed me over, but she had her reasons. Reasons I gave her. She wouldn't be in this mess if it weren't for the shit I did to her."

If there was one thing I knew in this world, it was people making judgements without knowing the full story. Growing up the black sheep of a good catholic family in a country town, I knew all about being judged. Fuck, I'd been tried and convicted in too many people's minds all my damn life. Always without evidence.

I nodded. "Whatever you need, you've got."

He lifted his chin towards the back of the house. "Go."

I left him, and when I rounded the corner of the house into the backyard, I dry retched at what I found out there. The filthy fuck who lived there, had left a dog chained up in the heat, and it's rotting body lay next to an empty bowl that I assumed once held water or food. Flies and maggots swarmed over the dog and the stench filled my nostrils.

Fucking assholes who did that kind of shit should be fucking shot as far as I was concerned.

I made my way to the back door, and when I found it locked, I lifted my boot and kicked hard, forcing it open. I entered the house through a dirty laundry jammed with putrid clothes and the kind of smell I was convinced could bring death to those who inhaled it.

Memories of my time living on the streets and in abandoned houses with filthy fuckers flooded my mind. A part of my life I'd rather forget. But even after twelve years, those memories were clear as day.

"Devil!" King roared from another room. "Need your help, brother."

I quickly found him in one of the bedrooms. King had a guy by the throat with his gun pointed to his head. A woman lay on the floor, her face full of bruises. Eyeing me, he said, "Devil, tell him what I like to do to men who beat their women up."

The guy's terrified eyes met mine. He'd be right to fear King. "He's been known to cut a guy's hands off for that."

King tightened his grip around the asshole's neck. When the guy grunted, the woman he'd been beating up whimpered on the floor next to the bed. I couldn't tell if she was scared for herself or for the guy. "I'm looking for Shannon Mercier. You know where he is?"

The guy shook his head. "No, and even if I did, I wouldn't fucking tell you."

"Fuck," I muttered. "Are you trying to get yourself hurt?"

His gaze met mine again. "Fucking cut my hands off. I'm not telling you where he is."

King let go of his throat. "Really? You'd give up your hands for him?"

The guy spat in King's face and opened his mouth to speak, but King punched him before he could utter a word.

As the asshole stumbled backwards, the woman cried out, "Marty!" She had enough sense to stay where she was, though, and leave King to his mission.

I shook my head at her. "Really? You're upset that the guy who beats you up is getting hurt?" Fuck, I'd never understand some women.

King ignored us, his attention solely on Marty. His entire body was taut with murderous energy as he bellowed, "You fucking spit in my face again and you'll lose your right hand. Now tell me, does Shannon mean that fucking much to you that you'd sacrifice body parts?"

"He's my fucking brother. I'm not giving him up."

"Figures," King said. "You both like to hit women. Your daddy teach you that shit?"

Marty bared his teeth. "Fuck you." Lunging at King, he attempted to wrap his arms around King's waist. However, he underestimated King, who always remained on high alert and anticipated what was to come.

"No, fuck you!" King roared as he raised his knee and jammed it up into Marty's chin. The force of his thrust knocked Marty onto his ass.

King moved swiftly behind him so he could grip his collar and drag him backwards. He slammed him against the wall, hard enough for his head to hit it and then bounce forward. He stared up at King through dazed eyes but didn't say a word. Blood streamed out of his mouth, coating his chin.

Crouching in front of him, King said, "Are we getting anywhere, Marty? Or do you need some more encouragement."

"Just tell him, Marty!" the woman screamed out. She'd scrambled her way up onto the bed, probably in an effort to escape King. At least one of them had some brains.

"Go to hell," Marty said, barely managing to get the words out.

King's mouth spread out into a wicked grin. Pulling his knife from its sheath, he said, "If anyone's going to hell today, it's you, not me." Pressing the tip of his blade to Marty's chest, he added, "I'll happily send you there if you don't give me what I want."

Marty's eyes widened as he realised where King was going with this. I doubted King would make good on that threat, though. If there was one thing he was really fucking good at, it was making people think his level of crazy meant he had no conscience, but I knew better. Sure, he'd done things in his life that most people would have nightmares from, but they weighed heavily on him. I'd been witness in the past to just how much. That was something, though, that I'd never tell another soul. It was King's private life, not mine to share. I wasn't sure if anyone else in the club had ever seen King the way I had, so most members bought into his crazy.

Marty's back pressed into the wall in an effort to move away from King, but he had nowhere to go. "Fuck, man, I can't—"

King dropped his knife beside him, took Marty's face in both hands and smashed his head backwards into the wall. "Stop fucking talking unless it's to give me some useful information."

"Wait! Don't kill him! I'll tell you what you want to know," the woman cried out. Marty grunted something unintelligible as he fought to move. King had put him in a world of hurt, though, and he was unable to push up off the floor.

Without a moment's hesitation, King swiped his knife off the floor and stalked to the bed. "Where is he?"

She stared up at him with fearful eyes. Her body was tense with anxiety. "You promise not to kill us?"

"Fuck, bitch," Marty muttered. "Shut the fuck up."

King gripped her hair at the back of her head. Yanking back on it, he said, "You give me what I want, and I won't touch another hair on either of your heads."

Ignoring Marty's desperate pleas to shut up, she said, "He's left Sydney. He found out you were looking for him, and he cleared out yesterday. Gone to Brisbane, I think."

Marty's "fuck" was enough to tell both of us that she wasn't lying. King let her go and glanced at me. "Looks like it's time to visit the Brisbane boys."

"You wanna leave today?"

He didn't reply, but rather motioned for me to follow him out of the house. When we stood outside at our bikes, he said, "I'm going to take Kick and Nitro with me. I want you to look after Jen while I'm gone."

I frowned. "Who does she need looking after from if the asshole who was hurting her is in Brisbane?"

"She's pregnant, Devil. I want you to make sure she stays that way."

***

"You should buy me a drink," I said to Tatum later that night when I found her and Monroe sitting at the bar at Flirt. I'd just checked in on Jen before heading to the pub to see if Hailee's band was playing.

Tatum's eyes met mine. Knowingly. "The band has just taken a break. They'll be back in about half an hour, but I think I saw Hailee floating around chatting with people, so you could go look for her now. And then if you still want a drink, I'll buy you one."

I grinned. "I like the way you think, Tatum."

Her gaze shifted to something behind me, and she lifted her chin. "Go. She just walked past us."

"I'll be back for that drink," I said before leaving her to go in search of Hailee.

I hadn't been able to get her out of my mind all week. Fuck, I'd even looked up the greyhound shit that she'd mentioned. And the more I thought about her, the more determined I was to spend time with her.

I followed her as she weaved in and out between people on her way to the corner of the pub where her bandmates sat. When I caught up with her, I reached for her arm and stopped her.

She spun around and met my gaze. "Devil." My name left her mouth on a gush of breathlessness, and I sensed her pleasure at seeing me again.

The crowded pub forced our bodies together, and I found myself going from mildly turned-on to completely fucking captivated. She consumed every one of my senses. The people around us failed to exist; my mind and body were focused entirely on her.

"Fuck, you're beautiful." Possibly not the best use of my time with her, but it captured her attention.

Her eyes lit up and she arched her back a little, which forced her tits closer to me. Biting her lip, she smiled and said, "And you're hot as sin and just as dangerous, I bet."

I had to fight with myself not to touch her. She was so damn close and so fucking sexy. Even in her sweaty just-performed state, she was sexy as hell to me. Images of her with sweat-slicked skin, her long hair stuck to it, hit me, and I groaned.

"What time do you finish tonight?"

"In about an hour or so. Why?"

"Because I'm buying you a drink tonight, and you're not gonna argue with me this time." I moved my mouth to her ear. "I don't give a fuck if you're kinda seeing someone. You spend some time with me, and I'll show you what it's like to not ever wanna flirt with any man but the man you're seeing."

I pulled my face away from hers and took in how her eyes had widened a fraction and the way her breathing had slowed. Her mouth formed a small O before she finally said, "I hate to break it to you, bossman, but I can't hang around tonight."

"Tomorrow then." *Bossman*. I fucking liked it.

"Nope, can't do that either."

"Pick a day, gorgeous, and I'll be here. But no way in hell am I taking no for an answer."

She stayed silent for a beat before exhaling a long breath. "I'm not trying to fob you off. I really do have stuff on tonight and tomorrow."

"You got a date tonight?"

"You just don't give up, do you?"

I pressed my body harder against hers. "No."

Staring at me, in what I presumed was either bewilderment or frustration, she ran her fingers through her hair and said, "I don't have a date tonight. The guy I'm seeing is actually out of town for a week or so. I have to go home and look after my grandmother tonight. She fell yesterday and hurt herself, so she needs someone there as often as possible to help her."

Her words wound themselves around me with an unfamiliar emotion. It was a mixture of happy surprise and respect. I didn't meet many people who commanded those emotions from me, so it felt a little surreal.

"You live with your grandmother?"

"Yes. Why?"

I smiled. "It's not often I meet people who live with their grandparents."

"Well, my grandfather was an asshole, so I never had anything to do with him. My grandmother lived with my parents, but when my dad died six months ago, I knew I couldn't leave her with my mum, so I moved her in with me."

"Your family sounds like it might be as dysfunctional as mine."

She checked her watch before glancing back up at me with a look of regret. "I really need to get a drink and freshen up before we go back on."

I placed my hand on her waist to keep her with me, half expecting her to pull out of my hold. She didn't, though, so I kept my hand there. "Name a day, Hailee."

I could have sworn her body swayed against mine when she said, "Sunday afternoon, around three. I'll meet you here for a drink."

I let her go. "I'll see you then."

As I watched her go, I realised she was the first woman in years I'd hounded for a date. Not that she'd probably call it a date, but I was going to. As far as I was concerned, our drink on Sunday would be the end of whatever the fuck she had going on with the guy she was seeing. And the beginning of something with me.

Chapter Six

Hailee

"Miss Hailee, how are you today?"

I smiled at the man who stood behind the counter of the convenience store waiting for my reply. "I'm good. And you, Avi? I was worried about you yesterday." I had been visiting this store at least once a day since my grandmother and I moved in to a house up the road six months ago. Avi and his wife, Preena, had become my friends in that time, and I'd been concerned when neither of them had been at the store the day before.

He waved away my worry. "Preena took ill, so I stayed home to look after her. She's much better today."

"I'm glad to hear that." I scribbled my phone number on a piece of paper from my bag and handed it to him. "I want you to call me if you ever need help with anything." I knew they had no family close by and not many friends. They'd called a friend in yesterday, but I wasn't sure how many people they had to rely on, so I wanted to help them in any way I could.

Avi gave me a huge smile. "Thank you, Miss Hailee. You have been very good to us."

"I haven't really done anything."

His eyes widened. "You have been like family to me and Preena. We can never thank you enough."

Sure, I'd helped them a few times when they'd been run off their feet, and I'd done a few other things here and there for them, but I didn't see this the same way he did. However, it made me feel like I may have done some good if he felt the way he did, so I gave him a smile and said, “There’s no need to thank me, Avi. It’s what friends do for each other.”

His phone rang, drawing him away from our conversation, so I turned to make my way to the fridges to grab some milk. I ran smack bang into a hard chest and a chuckle. Looking up, I found Devil smiling down at me.

“The places I run into you,” he murmured, seemingly happy that he had.

Pleasure at seeing him again ran through me, but I did my best to contain it. That was proving harder to do each time I saw him. The man was smoking hot and a huge flirt. He’d been wearing his cut tonight, which he hadn’t previously, so I discovered he was a member of the Storm MC. That should have been a warning, but it wasn’t. When I’d told him earlier that I’d meet for a drink in two days, I’d meant it.

“Do you live around here?” As soon as I said it, I realised it was probably a dumb question. The convenience store was just down the road from the pub, so he was probably on his way home.

“Yeah, about two blocks that way,” he said, pointing in the direction of his home. “Do you live close, too?”

I pointed in the opposite direction to his home. “I’m about a twenty-minute walk that way.”

“You’re walking home?” He seemed concerned, and my belly somersaulted at that. Having a man worry over me was something I hadn’t experienced in years.

Stop it, Hailee. You have Wayne.

“Yeah, my car’s out of rego and I can’t afford to pay for it for about two weeks, so I’m currently walking everywhere.” I smiled as I added, “It’s great exercise.” It irritated me that I always felt the need to tell people it was great exercise when I had to tell them why I couldn’t drive. But I was a little embarrassed about not being able to afford all my bills, and I deflected with the exercise comment.

"Fuck, it's not safe for you to be walking these streets at night."

"My brother sometimes drives me home, but he had to work tonight."

"And he's happy for you to walk?" He sounded incredulous.

"I may have told him I would cab it home." Aaron would hit the roof if he knew I walked home, but he also didn't know what it was like to be dirt poor. He was never short of cash. I could have asked him for a loan, but I didn't want to get even further behind in my bills.

"Right, grab your stuff and I'll walk you home," he said, taking charge in a bossy tone that, as much as I didn't want to admit, I liked. However, I'd never tell him that.

"I'm fine. I'm a big girl and I've done this walk many times in my life."

His eyes flashed with determination. "I know, but I don't care. Tonight you're doing it with me."

I stared at him. "We've just met and you wanna boss me around already?"

His eyes didn't let mine go. "Darlin', I'm betting you like me bossing you around. And to be honest, I like you arguing with me over it, so by all means, keep giving it to me, because I'll just keep giving it back."

He wasn't kidding. I didn't know him, but I figured that much about him so far. He didn't bullshit. I reached for a basket and yanked it up. "Oh, for God's sake," I muttered as if I was annoyed, but I wasn't. He was right—I liked the back and forth with him. But at the same time, I had an independent streak a mile wide, and no way in hell would I go down easily.

Without waiting for him, I walked to the fridges and grabbed milk and butter. I then stocked up on bread, Earl Grey teabags, and Tim Tams. My grandmother had an afternoon routine that consisted of tea and Tim Tams, and she'd be cranky if I forgot either of them tonight, because we'd run out during the day.

Devil stuck close behind me, but let me shop in silence. His presence alone caused a rush of butterflies in my tummy, though, and that put me off my game to the point that I dropped both the teabags and the Tim Tams while attempting to put them in my basket. And then when I bent to retrieve them, he did too, and we butted heads.

However, while I was in a state of nervous energy over it, he didn't appear to notice, being completely engrossed in concern for me. Reaching out, he placed his hand on my forehead. "You okay?"

"I'm fine." My voice was all breathy. God, what was happening to me tonight? I was like a damn schoolgirl around him.

I took the groceries out of his hand and dumped them in the basket before stalking back to the counter. I knew I was being all kinds of rude, but my thoughts and emotions were in a state of turmoil.

Confused as fuck was where I was at. Which was pretty much how I'd been since I'd met him. From that very first conversation we had in the back of Aaron's car, I'd been attracted to him. But I didn't want to be. I wanted to want Wayne, the predictable guy. However, I couldn't help myself around Devil. I flirted back every time he flirted. And I said yes to drinks before my brain caught up with my body. I was helpless to stop myself. The excitement I felt when he came near me was unlike anything I'd experienced before.

I paid for my items and chatted with Avi briefly before exiting the store. The summer heat hit me the moment I stepped foot outside, and I groaned my annoyance. Summer could fuck off; give me winter any day.

"Here, let me carry that," Devil said as he came up behind me and took the bag of groceries from me.

And there he went, surprising me by doing something most men I met didn't. "Old school manners. I like it," I said with a smile.

He fell into step with me as I walked along the footpath. "You don't make it through a childhood in a good catholic family without learning some manners along the way."

"Oh God, you too? The way you say 'make it through' leads me to believe you may have only just survived it."

He chuckled. "I made it through, but I'm not sure you could say I survived it."

"Same. Ruth Archer is not a woman you survive."

"That's your mum?"

"Yeah. She was a stay-at-home mother who excelled in all things wifely. Cooking, cleaning, raising a perfect family. She tried so hard to shape me to become just like her. Unfortunately, she failed, and all I became was one constant disappointment to her."

"So you're telling me you're *not* good at cooking and cleaning? I'm gonna have to rethink this whole chasing you thing now." The grin he watched me with almost caused me to trip over my own damn feet.

"If cooking and cleaning are what you're after, you've come to the wrong woman." I wanted to smack myself for flirting with him. Why the hell was I encouraging him?

"Darlin', cooking and cleaning can be learnt. The thing you have that I want can't be. I'm definitely not chasing the wrong woman."

I couldn't be sure, but I think my mouth dropped open at that. I wanted to shove it closed, but I was flat-out concentrating on putting one foot in front of the other while remembering to draw breath while I did it.

Finally, my brain caught up with my thoughts, and in an effort to change the subject, I blurted, "Tell me about your parents."

He didn't reply straight away. Instead, he took a moment before saying, "I haven't seen them for fifteen years. My father was ex-navy and strict, and my mother just went along with whatever he said. I loved her, but after a while, you wonder how you can love someone who allows bad shit to happen to their child."

I could hear the pain in his voice. His tone had turned from fun to hard, and it made me wonder what happened to him in his childhood. Devil had to be just over thirty, so fifteen years away from his parents would mean he left home in his teens.

The nurturer in me took over and I reached for his arm. I was never under the illusion I could fix things for people or take away their hurt, but the need to soothe compelled me to offer my touch. This often caused me trouble; a lot of people weren't comfortable with it and told me so. Or sometimes they didn't say anything, but they drew away from me.

Devil was different. He glanced down at my hand on his arm and then met my gaze. He didn't pull away and he didn't tell me to remove my hand. Rather, he said, "You wanna keep that up, I might not be able to restrain myself for much longer."

Although the street we walked along was lit only by the occasional streetlight, I could see the heat in his eyes. Or maybe it was that I could sense it, feel it. Devil didn't seem to be the kind of man to hide his feelings. They blazed brightly for all to see. I bet that most of the time he didn't even have to speak—his body language would probably be enough to convey his thoughts and emotions.

"I think you're lying," I said.

"How so?"

"Well, I know you've got manners and I know you were raised in a strict family, so I'm guessing that for all your talk, you're actually a man who *can* restrain himself and who treats women with respect. I don't think you'd ever make a move on a woman unless she signalled her readiness."

"And you don't think you've already signalled your readiness?"

I shook my head in mock exasperation. "I knew I shouldn't encourage you."

"And yet you did. That tells me everything I want to know, darlin'."

I didn't want to encourage him any further, so I shut up and walked the last few metres to my home in silence. Devil seemed to clue on to what I was doing and met my silence with that bloody grin of his that seemed to be permanently painted on his face.

He followed me up the few stairs we had to the front door and then down the hallway into the kitchen where he placed the groceries on the counter before saying, "For the record, you just looking at me encourages me, Hailee. But when you speak, it's like a whole other world I never knew opens up, and I want in on that world. And I don't give a fuck if that makes me sound like a fucking pussy. It's the truth."

My heart sped up to the point that I thought it would beat its way out of my chest. No man had ever said something like that to me before. My words sat in a big fat mess on my tongue, and I struggled with arranging them in a manner that they'd make sense if I said them.

My grandmother saved me the trouble of having to get my shit together when she entered the kitchen and cut in on our conversation. "It does make you sound like a fucking pussy, but hell if I wouldn't have fallen for that when I was Hailee's age. She'd be a damn fool not to give you a chance."

Oh. God.

Jean Archer had a way with words, that was for damn sure.

Devil chuckled as he glanced at her. "I can see where Hailee gets her sass from."

Without thinking, I flung my hand out and lightly smacked him on the chest. Our eyes met as I said, "I'm nowhere near as sassy as my grandmother, thank you."

His chuckle turned into a belly laugh and he grabbed my hand before I could pull it back. Holding it against his chest, he said, "Maybe I should take your grandmother out for a drink on Sunday instead."

It was my turn to laugh. "She'd probably love that." I turned to her. "You do love your gin after all."

Devil's hand on mine was doing crazy shit to my body, and I attempted to pull away, but he shook his head and mouthed, "No" before looking at my grandmother again. "How about it, Gran? You up for drinks with me and Hailee on the weekend?"

She narrowed her eyes at him and tsked. "I know what you're doing, young man. Trying to get into my granddaughter's pants through me. You're shit out of luck there, though. You want in, you're gonna have to do the work yourself."

I couldn't believe she'd just said that. But I should have, because she'd never been one to beat around the bush in her life.

Well, except when it came to my mother. She'd beaten around that bush for decades.

"Jesus, Gran," I muttered as I pulled my hand away from Devil's. "Do you have to be so to the point?"

She scowled at me as she hobbled around the kitchen with her cane. Her seventy-five years were catching up to her, and she was slowly starting to lose her health, but she had her wits about her still. "Life's too damn short to fuck around, my dear. More people should just say it like it is, and then we'd all know where we stand." I knew this was coming from all those years of her trying like hell to get my mother to like her, with no success. The minute my mother turned on her completely after my father died, Gran hardened a little more and began speaking bluntly to everyone. I usually appreciated it, but with Devil, for some reason, I felt a little ruffled that she'd speak so openly to him.

I shouldn't have been concerned, though. He took it in his stride. Even seemed to welcome it. "Life *is* too damn short to fuck around. I agree. And yes, I was trying to get into Hailee's pants through you, but I see that's not going to work for me here. I appreciate the heads up. I'll shift gears now and try other avenues."

Gran nodded. I shook my head. "Really? You two are gonna stand here and talk about me as if I'm not even in the room?"

"Feel free to leave," my grandmother said.

Devil's lips twitched in amusement. "I'm gonna leave you two alone now. Maybe your grandmother can talk some sense into you," he said with a wink.

I rolled my eyes and shooed him into the hallway. "Maybe she'll tell me I should look for a man who's not a fucking pussy."

He stopped and turned, backing me up against the wall. He placed one hand on the wall above me and the other around my waist. Pressing himself into me, he growled, "You feel that, darlin'? That's what's waiting for you when you're ready to acknowledge how much you fucking want me." He bent his mouth to my ear and added, "When you're ready to leave behind a man who doesn't even have the fucking balls to tell me to back the fuck off when I'm watching you like I wanna run my tongue through your pussy before I fuck you into unconsciousness."

My legs turned to jelly.

I forgot how to breathe.

No words came.

I was a mess.

An achy, needy mess.

Devil let me go, and I watched as he walked the short distance down the hallway to the front door. He exited the house without a backwards glance at me, which was a good fucking thing. If he had looked back, he would have seen how desperately I wanted to beg him to come back.

"I like that man," my grandmother said, causing me to jump.

I stood straight and ran my fingers through my hair. My senses were scrambled, and I fought to unscramble them. "Huh?"

"I said, I like that man. He has some fire to him. You should dump Wayne and date him. What's his name? You never did introduce us."

"That's because you two were busy with your conversation," I muttered.

She stared at me. "Well, his name?"

God how I loved her, even when she was bossy and cantankerous. "Devil."

Her forehead crinkled in a frown. "Devil? What kind of name is that?"

"It's his nickname. I don't know his real name."

She hobbled back into the kitchen, throwing over her shoulder, "Find out his name. I want to know what it is. And invite him to dinner next week. I'll cook."

My eyes widened. She never cooked anymore. Hadn't in the time we'd lived together. I'd begged her numerous times, because she was the best cook I knew, but she always fobbed me off with an excuse.

"Only if you cook roast pork," I called out, holding my breath. She didn't like roast pork, but she used to cook it for our family, and hers was the only one I loved. I could practically taste the pork crackling while I stood waiting for her reply. I'd invite Devil over, encouraging him further, against all my better judgement, just for her crackling.

"You buy it, I'll cook it."

Oh. God.

Devil was coming for dinner.

Chapter Seven

Devil

"You don't like that King is looking after me, do you?" Jen said early the next morning when I dropped in to check on her.

I rubbed the back of my neck. Not a conversation I wanted to get into. Especially not at eight in the morning, after only a few hours sleep. I'd spent half the night thinking about Hailee, finally jerking off to those thoughts at around three and then falling asleep.

"It's none of my business what King does," I said, taking in her exhausted state. She'd looked tired the night before also, and I wondered if she'd had any sleep at all.

She ushered me into the house, and I followed her into the lounge room. Sitting on the couch, she curled her legs under her and rested against the arm of the chair. "It mightn't be your business what he does, but if you're gonna come over every day and check on me for him, I'd prefer you to not look at me like you'd rather be anywhere else but here. And I'm guessing you do that because you don't like me."

I sat on the edge of the couch opposite her and rested my elbows on my legs. "I don't know you enough to decide whether I like you or not, Jen. But yeah, I guess I've formed an opinion of what you did to King all those years ago. Leaving a man for another man isn't high on my list of honourable things to do."

She watched me silently for a beat. "No, I guess it isn't. But you don't know the full story, so I really wish you wouldn't form an opinion."

Fuck, again, not a conversation I wanted to be having. Ever. What King chose to do in his life had nothing to do with me. He could have allowed his women to fuck around all they wanted on him and I wouldn't have cared.

I stood. "Do you need anything? I can swing by later and drop it off if you do."

She joined me. "I loved King, still do. I would never have left him if he hadn't given me good reason to, Devil."

"Yeah, King said as much."

"But you didn't believe him?"

"Look, Jen, honestly I don't care what went on between you two. And I don't care that you're back together n—"

"We're not together."

Her words caught me by surprise. I didn't know why I thought that because they were having a child together, they'd stay together, but I had. I'd figured that'd be King's style.

She must have clued on to the thoughts running through my mind. "I'm not pregnant with King's child."

I stared at her. There was another guy involved? Fuck, I was way over this conversation. "Okay."

She grabbed hold of my arm as I turned to leave, stopping me. "The guy that I left King for? The one who was hitting me… he found me again…" She let me go and covered the sob escaping from her mouth. Tears slid down her cheeks as she tried to get herself under control. Her efforts were in vain, though. A moment later, tears gushed down her face and her body crumpled.

I caught her and held her while she sobbed. I didn't say anything, but rather waited for her to cry it out, at which point I hoped that she'd just want me to leave without ending the conversation we'd been having.

No such luck.

She pulled out of my hold and wiped her face. "This baby is his." She paused for a moment. "He forced himself on me about a month and a half ago. I didn't tell King because I didn't want to drag him into it any more than he already was. I really didn't want to cause him any more problems. The only reason he found out that Shannon was still threatening me was because my friend rang him about it."

"He knows it's not his, right?"

"Yes, absolutely. And I never told Shannon I was pregnant."

Thank fuck King knew this. I'd hate to see what he'd do if he thought the baby was his, only to discover later it wasn't.

"King's a good man," I murmured, deep in thought. I wasn't sure too many men I knew would do what he was for Jen.

She nodded and wrapped her arms around her body. "He is," she said softly, her voice cracking a little. "I just wish things could have been different between us."

"You're not going to do anything crazy, are you?" I remembered the way King had said he wanted Jen to stay pregnant. Looking at her, all I saw was despair, and I had to wonder how her mental state was.

Sighing deeply, she said, "I'm not going to do anything crazy. I know King thinks I am, but I won't. This baby may not have been conceived in love, but it doesn't deserve to die because of that."

"Yeah, that's true." Fuck, what a fucked-up situation. No wonder King was on a rampage to find this motherfucker.

"I'm sorry to drag you into all this."

Something told me that as much as she made that conversation about my opinion of her to begin with, what she really wanted was someone to talk to. I couldn't blame her.

"King gave you my number, right?" At her nod, I continued, "Call me whenever you need to, okay?"

Her eyes widened a touch—in surprise, by the looks of it. "Thank you," she whispered, and I noted the tears that leaked from her eyes.

I nodded before turning and leaving. I still didn't understand the whole King-and-Jen dynamic, but like I'd said to her, I didn't need to. But fuck, to carry a child who was the product of rape, and to say what she'd said about that child... Jen had my respect for that.

***

Saturday passed way too fucking slowly. I couldn't get Hailee out of my mind, so to pass time until I saw her, I decided to head over to my sister-in-law's and hang out there.

"Are you psychic?" Sonya asked when she opened her door to me mid-afternoon. "These kids are driving me crazy, and I think that uncle time is just what they need."

I grinned, stepping inside her house. "You wanna go out for the afternoon?"

As I made the short trek into her kitchen, I noticed the messy state of the place. Strange, because Sonya was a neat freak. Lego, dolls, and other toys littered the living room, and dirty dishes were stacked in a chaotic fashion in the kitchen.

"No, can you just play with the kids for a bit while I clean up? Adam has been sick the last couple of days, so I haven't had a chance to do anything."

"Fuck, Sonya, you should have called me to come over. When does Campbell get back?" Campbell was my brother and worked away from home most of the time with the navy.

"Oh, God, he's not home for another three weeks." Exhaustion and stress filled her voice, and I decided it was way past time for me to step in.

"Uncle Dominic!" Kylie squealed when she caught sight of me and threw herself into my arms.

I held her and pressed a kiss to her forehead. "Hey, princess. What you up to?"

Her tiny mouth spread out into the biggest smile. God, she was precious. The last four years with her in my life had been some of the best years I'd known. When she was a baby, I used to lie next to her for hours while she slept. Just watching her. Making sure no harm came to her in her sleep. While they could be loud and demanding, children were so fucking peaceful. They didn't yet carry the baggage of hate and fear and hurt and distrust and doubt. And while they often had a temper, they didn't yet know anger.

Threading her little fingers through my hair, she gripped a few strands and said, "I wanna play on the swing!"

"Okay, we'll take Adam and go outside to play while Mummy cleans up inside." Sonya gave me a look of complete relief and thanks.

Kylie began kicking her legs in excitement. "Put me down! Put me down! I'll get Adam."

I let her go and watched as she ran out of the room in search of her brother. Glancing at Sonya, I said, "You do what you need to do here, and then I'm taking everyone out for dinner so you don't have to cook."

"Thank you, Dom. I honestly don't know what I'd do without you most of the time."

"You'd get by." And she would. Sonya was a strong woman. I just liked to be able to help her where I could.

"Yeah, but Campbell wouldn't recognise me when he came home from sea. I'd be a messy, grumpy wife. Maybe even an alcoholic, too."

"You wouldn't be. You don't have time to drink."

She laughed. "True!"

Kylie came back into the kitchen, her brother in tow. Two years younger than her, Adam was often dragged around by his sister. He adored her, though, and never complained. She grabbed my hand. "Let's go!"

I allowed her to pull me with her and a couple of moments later, we were at the swing in the backyard. I'd bought it for the kids a couple of weeks ago, and it had fast become Kylie's favourite thing to do. Sonya both loved and hated me for that swing.

We spent the next hour playing outside. After they'd had enough of the swing, we kicked a ball around for a while, and then I chased them around the yard in an effort to wear them out for Sonya. When we went back inside, we found their mother asleep on her bed.

"Shh," I said to them with my finger against my lips. Once I'd herded them out of the bedroom, I quietly closed the door and led the kids to the living room. Change of plans for the night. "Who wants macaroni and cheese for dinner?" I knew it was one of their favourites, and I knew how to cook it. They both squealed their delight, and when I added, "After dinner, we'll watch a movie, your choice," they were completely sold on leaving their mother to sleep. And I managed to hold my title of favourite uncle for another day.

Chapter Eight

Hailee

As I entered the pub on Sunday afternoon, I adjusted the straps on my dress. It was hot as hades, so I'd worn a short flowy black dress to meet Devil for drinks. I'd paired it with flat sandals, which was not my usual style, but in this heat, I just wanted comfort and air on my skin.

I'd spent the weekend going back and forth in my mind between Devil and Wayne. My brain had whiplash over it, and I was thankful to be seeing Devil that afternoon. Perhaps spending time with him would push my mind in the right decision. The thing was, I knew it was my fear holding me back more than anything. And fear needed to be banished from my life. I'd worked hard over the last two years not to let it in, so I'd be damned if I did now.

Scanning the pub, I found Devil kicking back on a lounge, watching me with those eyes that told me how much he wanted to fuck me. He wore jeans with a black fitted T-shirt and a wicked smile. Jesus, the man was sin personified.

He didn't stand to meet me, just waited where he was, not moving an inch. His eyes moved, though. All over me. So much so that when I finally stood in front of him, my carefully constructed thoughts about how I'd handle him were flailing helplessly. No way would today go the way I planned. Devil had taken charge without even uttering a damn word.

He did stand when I met him at the lounge. His hand slid easily around my waist, and he pulled me close so he could place his mouth near my ear. It seemed to be his favourite thing to do.

Possibly because he'd worked out that it put me off my game. "Anyone ever tell you how sexy you look in that dress?"

I pressed a hand to his chest. His rock-hard chest. His chest that I wanted to get a glimpse of. Fuck, I needed to keep my thoughts in check. Pushing him away, I found his gaze again. "I can't say they have."

His hand lingered on my waist. "That's a damn shame. A woman like you should hear that all the time."

Guilt washed over me as I basked in his compliment. There was no more denying it—I liked Devil. More than I liked Wayne. It was time to end whatever it was I had going with Wayne, because I was definitely not the type of woman to lead a man on. Or the kind of woman to cheat on a man. Regardless of where this ended up with Devil, Wayne was not the man for me.

Devil's eyes narrowed at me. "What are you thinking, darlin'? Looks serious."

"I was thinking that you should get me a French Martini. And that I want to know everything there is to know about you."

His fingers dug into my skin at my waist and he lowered his mouth to my ear again. "You wanna know what *my* thoughts were?" At my nod, he said, "I was thinking about how much I want to fuck you with my tongue."

Burning hot need slid through me, straight to my core. I squeezed my legs together at the same time that I ran my hand down his chest and gripped the side of his shirt. When our eyes met again, I said, "I was thinking more along the lines of you fucking me with your cock, but we could begin with your tongue."

"Fuck," he hissed.

I let him go. "You should go get the drinks so we can get started."

He did, and when he returned, I'd kicked off my sandals and settled on the lounge with my legs tucked under me. Sunday afternoons were for comfort as far as I was concerned.

Devil returned, and I watched in fascination as he folded his body onto the lounge next to me. I'd never been with a man who was as built as he was. My eyes were glued to him—his ass, then his legs, his thighs—oh, God how I imagined them in bed—his chest and finally, his arms. It was like muscle heaven.

Lifting a bottle of beer to his mouth, he spread an arm across the back of the lounge behind me and drew my attention back to his face. "Say the word, gorgeous, and we'll get out of here. I'm all yours."

In an effort to buy some time and find my words again, I took a sip of the cocktail he'd bought me. The thought of having all of him—every inch of his body—made my pulse speed.

He'd twisted slightly so he faced me. He was so damn close I fought the urge to run my fingers over his lips. Instead, I said, "You're intent on driving me insane with lust, aren't you?"

"Is that what I'm doing?"

"Yes, but I'm guessing you already know that."

He leaned even closer, his eyes fixed firmly on mine. "I don't know anything for sure with you, Hailee."

While Devil was fun and flirty, every now and then he gave me a glimpse of the intensity I was beginning to think burned through him. I'd sensed a dangerous undertone to him before, and I wondered how deep it ran.

I decided to let him in on my thoughts. Playing with men wasn't my style. "I'm not going to see Wayne anymore."

Approval flared in his eyes. "Good."

"And my grandmother wants you to come to dinner one night during the week."

A smile touched his lips. "I'm free any night. You tell me which one and I'll be there."

I wasn't sure what I'd expected, but it wasn't the easiness of his reply. I still couldn't work out if he was a player or not. His smooth manner made me think he was, but everything else about him made me feel like he was chasing me for more than sex.

I decided to be completely upfront with my thoughts. "Are you just after sex here? I mean, if you are, I'm on board with that, but I'd rather know going in what this is rather than thinking it could be more when that's not what you're thinking."

He smiled harder and leant forward so he could kiss me. His lips on mine blazed a line of hunger along my skin. I wanted more. And he didn't disappoint.

Parting my lips, he deepened the kiss, his tongue searching for mine. He took my face in his hands, and his body slid across the lounge towards mine until we were touching.

I wanted to crawl into his lap and never let him end this kiss.

I wanted to rip his shirt off and put my hands all over his body.

God, I wanted to do so many dirty things to him—things I'd never done to another man, but had dreamt of.

"Darlin'," he rasped, pulling his mouth from mine, which made me want to cry out my disappointment. "We need to stop this now or else I'm not gonna be able to stop. I'd happily fuck you on this lounge if it's what you wanted, but I doubt it is."

I took hold of his face. "I need your lips on mine for at least another five minutes, and if you can't control yourself, that's on you." My words came out on a huff of bossy breathlessness, because that was what a kiss from Devil did to me. I could only imagine what sleeping with him would do. Hell, he might cause me to stop breathing all together.

His eyes widened a fraction before he grinned. “Jesus, you’re something else, woman.”

And then he gave me what I wanted.

And I knew what his answer would be about whether this was just sex or not.

This was never going to just be about sex.

***

“Your pussy tastes sweeter than I imagined,” Devil said as he moved his way up my body, pressing kisses to as much of my skin as he could along the way.

After just over an hour at Flirt, driving each other crazy for sex, he’d leant over and growled in my ear, “I’m done, here. I want you on the back of my bike, and then I want you on your back. And don’t think for a second that you’ll be leaving my place before tomorrow.”

I hadn’t argued, because what woman would ever disagree with a man like Devil when he took charge like that?

Meeting his gaze as his face came closer to mine, I said, “You imagined what it would taste like?”

He positioned his body over mine, his hard cock teasing me. Devil had gotten me naked faster almost than I could blink. I’d hardly had time to take a look at his home before he’d undressed me. That was pretty much as soon as he closed his front door behind us.

Once he had me naked, he’d thrown me over his shoulder and walked us into his lounge room. He’d rummaged in a cupboard for a blanket, thrown it on the lounge room floor, and positioned me in the middle of it. I’d watched, transfixed, as he’d stripped. Every glorious inch of his body had been revealed to me, and I'd been like a kid at Christmas, practically bouncing with excitement to find out exactly what was inside my present.

Devil really was like a present. An exquisitely wrapped one with his beautifully inked skin. I'd only had a taste of what was inside, and I needed more. I wanted to know everything that was inside this man. His thoughts, feelings, hopes, regrets, flaws, strengths, weaknesses, talents, disappointments, successes… all of the things that made him who he was.

And that frightened me a little, because I knew I was the kind of person who didn't do things by halves. When I was in, I was all in, and it scared people off. It certainly scared men off. I couldn't count the number of guys I'd started dating who had fled the minute I wanted everything all at once. I had tried to change this about myself, but I couldn't change the one thing about me that caused it—I felt things on such a deep level that they consumed me. And I'd never found a man who could handle that.

Devil dipped his mouth to mine and kissed me before saying, "Since the moment we met, I haven't *stopped* thinking about what you'd taste like."

I wrapped my arms and legs around him. "Seriously, every word out of your mouth gets me wetter. You could probably just keep talking and I'd come."

He grinned. "We'll have to test that theory out one day, but not today. Today I've got other plans."

"I hope they include your tongue inside me again." *Oh, God, please say yes.*

"They include more than just that inside you, darlin'."

I let him go as he pushed up, and then I watched in anticipation as he lowered his lips to my pussy again.

His eyes held mine as he licked slowly from one end to the other, before sucking my clit into his mouth.

My back arched.

My arms flung out and gripped the blanket.

Fuck, yes.

Yes, yes, yes.

I closed my eyes as the pleasure he gave rippled through me. It started out small and grew in intensity until every last cell in my body sung with adoration for everything that was Devil.

His tongue.

His lips.

His hands.

And his God-given talent for using all those things together in the way I was pretty sure God meant them to be used. Well, maybe not, but I was, again, almost certain every woman on earth would agree with me there.

As he brought me closer to orgasm, a chant I had no control over fell from my mouth. A combination of his name and God's name and a few swear words. I could hardly hear myself over the rush of bliss roaring through me, but I knew words were flowing.

When I finally fell over the edge and lingered in that divine space of pleasurable nothingness, Devil's strong hands moved along my body, up to my waist where he gripped me with one hand while the other one slid up my back to take hold of my neck. He pulled me to a sitting position, bringing our mouths together. Nipping my bottom lip with his teeth, he rasped, "Listening to you say my name over and over has my dick so fucking hard."

I opened my eyes to find him staring at me, full of need. Reaching for his cock, I said, "It's my turn now."

He stopped me with a shake of his head, his hand pushing mine away from its destination. "No, darlin', I need in this sweet pussy. You can suck my dick later, but right now, I'm gonna come inside of you."

Before I had a chance to respond, he had me on my back with my legs spread while he reached for a condom in his wallet.

"I honestly figured you for a guy who'd fuck me from behind, maybe with your hand around my throat," I said, watching his muscles flex as he moved. Goddam, he was gorgeous. My pussy clenched, desperate to have him inside.

He took hold of his cock and ran it through my wetness before rubbing the tip of it over my clit. Over and over in a delicious rhythm that caused my body to arch up again.

His eyes met mine, dark with desire. "That'll come, but the first time I fuck you"—he pushed his cock inside me, not far, but enough for me to miss it when he pulled back out—"I wanna watch your face while I stamp my name on your tongue." He caught my lips in a long, deep kiss, and then added, "I'm going to show you how it feels to be fucked by a man who is so fucking caught up in you that all he can think about is you and when he'll next get to see you. You ever had that, darlin'?"

Oh, fuck, I had never had that. I was sure of it, because I'd never felt the way Devil made me feel. He'd lit a fire in me, and it had spread from my mind to my core and out to my fingertips and toes.

I couldn't think straight.

I couldn't process my feelings.

All I saw was him.

All I felt was him.

And all I knew, right then, was *him.*

"No," I whispered, "I've never had that."

He growled as he entered me, and it vibrated through my body, setting off another round of extreme pleasure. My breaths turned into pants when he started fucking me. Good God, his dick was huge. I'd never been filled so well. It was exquisite, and worked me into such a state that I found myself clawing my fingernails into his skin while I begged him to fuck me harder. Rougher.

With his body on top of me and my limbs around him, his eyes clung to mine. "You want it harder?"

I dug my fingers into his back. "Yes."

He pulled out and then slammed his dick into me harder. "More?" The word left his lips on another growl. The kind of deep, masculine sound that did all kinds of good shit to me.

I wondered how much harder he could give it to me. Tightening my arms around him, I demanded, "Yes, more."

"Fuck," he roared as he gave me everything he had.

I'd never been fucked the way Devil was fucking me. It was rough and dirty, and I couldn't get enough. He gave me the whole experience—his dick pounding into me, eyes that never left mine, a powerful body that commanded my attention, guttural sounds that told me how into me he was, and dominance that excited me.

He took me on a ride I never wanted to get off, and when my toes curled and my core quivered, and I came, I knew I'd do anything to have him again. Devil had made good on his promise. He'd stamped his name on my tongue. Hell, he'd engraved himself all over me, so much so that I wasn't sure I'd ever look at another man again.

Chapter Nine

Devil

My phone woke me the next morning, dragging me from the best fucking dream I'd ever had. Hailee featured in it, and for all my efforts to stay with it, the fucking phone made sure I didn't.

I flung my arm out towards the bedside table in search of my phone but failed in my attempt. When it stopped ringing, I gave up and reached for Hailee.

I found an empty bed.

What the fuck?

I thought for sure she'd still be here after the night we had last night. And it wasn't the sex that blazed front and centre in my mind. It was the way she managed to make me anticipate what was to come between us. I hung off every word she said, every smile she sent my way, the way she saw everything. The thrill of not knowing what I was gonna get from her next could become an addiction. I wanted to sit and talk with her for hours. I wanted to reach deep into her mind so I could know her. *Really* know her.

I wanted to see the parts of her she showed no one else.

Leaving my bed, I threw on some shorts, brushed my teeth and headed out to the kitchen. I needed coffee. And hopefully I'd find Hailee there, too.

She wasn't in the kitchen, but I did find her in the lounge room. I slowed as she came into view when I entered the room. She sat cross-legged on the blanket I'd spread across the floor the night before, with her hands resting on her knees and her eyes closed. I wasn't sure, but she appeared to be meditating.

Resting my shoulder against the wall, I crossed my arms in front of me while I watched her. I loved that she had thrown one of my tees on. There was something about seeing a woman who did crazy good shit to you, in your clothes.

A good few minutes passed before she said, "Morning." She didn't stop what she was doing, though. She simply carried on in silence after taking a moment to acknowledge my presence.

"Mornin', darlin'. You do this every morning?"

She nodded and murmured, "Yeah."

I pushed off from the wall. "I don't want to interrupt you. I'm gonna make coffee. You want one?"

She turned then and hit me with a smile that woke every part of me up. "I'd love a coffee, thank you."

Her legs unfolded and she spread them out in front of her, drawing my attention there. The only thing in my mind after that was the memory of those legs hugging me last night.

As I stood staring at her legs, lost in thought, her soft laughter floated through the air. "Am I not getting coffee now?"

My eyes found hers again. "Yeah, but as soon as you're finished in here, I want your ass in the kitchen." Without waiting for her to reply, I walked out of the room.

Christ, it was hard to take those steps when all I wanted to do was bend her over and fuck her again. But I also wanted to give her the space to finish whatever it was she'd been doing.

"Devil."

My step faltered at the sound of her right behind me. Spinning around, we came face-to-face.

Hailee was fucking perfect.

Even first thing in the morning when her mascara from the night before was a little smudged and her hair a little messy.

Especially first thing in the morning.

I ran my finger down her cheek and along her jaw. Holding her eyes, I said, "Why do you wear so much makeup when you're fucking beautiful without it?"

Her lips curled as she smiled. That smile made it all the way to her eyes, too, as she reached for my waist. Her fingers ghosted over my skin lightly before she gripped me. Moving closer, she stood on her toes and planted a good-morning kiss on my mouth.

Hailee's morning kisses were something I was going to work hard to experience on a regular basis. She didn't stop at one; she kept going until our bodies melded together, our arms clung to each other and we were breathless. She tasted like toothpaste, and I loved that she'd felt comfortable enough to use my stuff.

When she finished kissing me and tried to pull away, I grabbed my tee she wore and pulled her back to me. My other hand held her ass as I said, "You don't think a man could be satisfied with a few kisses, do you?"

She slid a hand over my shoulder and up into my hair at the back of my neck. "I'm dying for a coffee. I've been awake for at least an hour, and believe me when I tell you that if I don't get caffeine in the morning, I'm a grumpy bitch."

I gripped her ass harder. "First, you might be dying for coffee, but *I'm* dying for pussy. Second, why the fuck didn't you wake me an hour ago? I could have had my fill, and you could be on your way to caffeine. And third"—I dipped my mouth to her neck and sucked her there for a moment before glancing up—"I'd like to see the grumpy, bitchy side of you. I think it'd get my dick even harder for you."

She moved her hands so she could push against my chest. "I hate to break it to you, bossman, but I have to go to work today. There's no pussy worshipping time available to you this morning."

As I let her go, I said, "You're fucking killing me here, Hailee. How long do I have?"

"You have the time it takes you to make me a coffee and talk to me for fifteen minutes. Then I have to go home so I can get ready."

"Your take-charge attitude turns me on, but let's remember who's the boss here." Truth be told, I could go all day with her trying to boss me.

She lifted a brow. "*Let's* remember who has the pussy here."

I snaked my arm around her waist and yanked her back to me. Bending my mouth to her ear, I growled, "And let's remember just how wet that pussy is for me. I'll give you your coffee and conversation this morning, but to be clear, you're back in my bed tonight, and my dick *will* be deep inside you more than once."

Her breaths came faster at that. Finding my eyes again after I let her go, she said, "Damn, you are demanding."

"I am. Now move that sweet ass into my kitchen so I'm not wasting a minute of the time I have left with you this morning."

She did as I said, and a minute later, I had her sitting on my kitchen counter while I made us coffee. Her legs dangled over the edge while she leant back and rested her hands behind her. I loved how at home she looked. How at ease she seemed with me already.

"How long have you been with Storm?"

I filled the kettle and spooned coffee into mugs. "Seven years."

"How old were you then?"

"Twenty-five."

"What made you join? Like, did you grow up around the club?"

I rested my ass against the counter and folded my arms over my chest while I waited for the kettle to boil and contemplated sharing the truth of my story with Hailee. I didn't usually tell it to anyone and especially not women I wanted to sleep with, but I already knew I wanted something with her. And if she couldn't accept my club ties, we had no chance at anything.

"You sure you wanna know that story, darlin'? It's probably not one you'd like."

"If there's one thing I've learnt in my thirty years, it's that perfection doesn't exist. Everyone's story is filled with imperfection. And who am I to judge yours?"

"Why the fuck did it take us so long to meet? I've been going to that pub for years, and not once have I seen you play there."

She smiled. "I think we meet people when we're supposed to. When we need them."

I uncrossed my arms and let them drop to my sides. "That seems like very fucking woo-woo-out-there kinda shit. I'm not sure I buy into that. What about the people we meet that are assholes? What do we need them for?"

Her smile grew. "Maybe they need us. Maybe they'll teach us a lesson, in which case we do need them."

The kettle boiled at that point, and I turned to make coffee. "Milk? Sugar?"

"Just a tiny splash of milk, please. No sugar." I heard her feet hit the floor, and a moment later, her arm slid around my waist. "So will you tell me your story about Storm, or will I have to wait for that?" She paused for a second. "Just so you know, I'm down for waiting. We've got all the time to get to our stories."

I turned my face to look at her. "Yeah, we do," I murmured. "I think I might leave that one for another day." She really wasn't ready for that one.

The smile on her face seemed to have settled there. "Okay, you've gotta give me three things about you, then. Anything. And then I'll give you three things about me."

Shifting on my feet, I turned my body to face her. I loved that she kept her hand on my waist. "What shit do you wanna know, gorgeous?"

She thought about that for a minute, and then her smile morphed into a grin. "Tell me your favourite movie."

That was an easy one. Growing up, we'd watched it over and over to the point I could recite it along with the characters. "*The Karate Kid*."

"You surprise me, Devil. I thought for sure you were gonna say some violent action flick. Any others?"

I had to dig deep, because I didn't watch movies often. "What's the name of that one with that chick from the movie with the bus that the guy from *The Matrix* was in? The chick from the bus movie takes in a poor kid who goes on to become a top football player."

She laughed and shook her head. "Your clues are a mess, dude, but it's *The Blind Side*. And it's Sandra Bullock who stars in it."

"Good flick. Fucking loved her character." I pulled her closer to me. "What are your favourites?"

"My absolute favourite movie ever is *Marley and Me*."

"The dog flick, yeah?"

"Yes."

"Guaranteed to make any chick bawl." I made a mental note to watch it with her simply for the opportunity to get her in my arms when she started crying.

She nodded and her hand squeezed my waist as she said, "Okay, favourite thing to do on a Sunday."

"Why a Sunday?"

"Because that's our rest day."

"Fuck, are you a happy clapper?"

Laughing, she said, "I'm not sure. What's a happy clapper?"

"A religious nut."

"Ah, I see the math you did there. Rest day, religion. I believe in God, but I'm not into church or any of that, if that's what you mean. When I talk about rest day, I just mean that I personally believe in taking one day a week and doing nothing but things you love."

It was my turn to smile. "So the fact you chose to hang out with me yesterday was a good sign that you really like me?"

She reached for my face and angled it down so she could kiss me. "You should most definitely take that as a good sign."

I warred with myself over the desire to keep her lips on mine versus the desire to finish this conversation. In the end, I decided I wanted to know shit about her more than I wanted a few minutes kissing her. "Okay, tell me your favourite things for a Sunday."

"Well, besides having drinks with hot bikers, I love to go out dancing or to see a live band. A lazy sleep in is always a good way to start the day, and time with friends shopping and having lunch is always good, too."

I narrowed my eyes at her. "When you say drinks with hot bikers, plural, that was just a slip of the tongue, wasn't it?"

Her body swayed against mine a little as she softly laughed at that. "Of course. There's only one hot biker I know. The rest aren't hot."

We needed to move away from this topic. Usually, I had a good sense of humour and could handle teasing like this, but with Hailee, I was experiencing a weird rush of territorial bullshit. I'd always lived with the belief that if the person you were with wanted someone else, then so be it; you weren't meant to be. I hadn't ever really experienced jealousy. Suddenly, jealousy was crawling all over me, and I didn't know what to do with it.

I reached for the coffee I'd made and passed it to her. "What are you doing tonight?"

Taking a sip, she looked at me over the rim of the mug. "Are you trying to change the subject? You haven't told me your favourite Sunday things yet."

This conversation I could handle. I grinned. "Darlin', there're only two things a Sunday should be reserved for. A long ride and sex."

"You're not a Sunday armchair sportsman, then?"

"Armchair sports are best watched in bed while balls deep in a sweet pussy, but I have been known to watch some motor racing or footy with the boys. A coldie in front of the telly is always a good thing on a Sunday afternoon."

She moved her hand from my waist to my chest. "Just putting it out there that I'm not the kind of woman who shares my cock time with a bloody television, so don't go getting any ideas that I'll put up with you watching sport while we have sex."

My dick twitched at her declaration. Mostly because her attempts at ordering me around got me hard, but also because that declaration told me she also planned for us to be something. I drank some of my coffee before saying, "I like the way you think. Sex first and then television."

"Or maybe, just sex. Hours and hours of it. And no television."

I grinned again. "Even fucking better."

She finished her coffee and said, "Okay, bossman, I gotta leave."

I stopped her as she took a step away from me. "Not until you agree to see me tonight."

"The band always plays at Flirt on a Monday. We could hang out after."

"What time do you start?"

"Eight tonight."

"I'll see you then."

She planted another kiss on my lips, driving me crazy because I needed more than one quick kiss from her. When she pulled away, I said, "I'll take you home."

Surprise flickered over her face. "I was just gonna walk."

I frowned. "Fuck no."

A slow smile crept across her face as she looped her hands around my neck. "In that case, I don't have to leave so soon. I can stay for another half hour."

My arms snaked around her so I could take hold of her ass. Lifting her, I turned and deposited her on the kitchen counter. "Thank fuck, because I've got at least half-an-hour worth of things I wanna do to you before I let you go." Without wasting another second, I dropped my mouth to hers. It was going to be the longest day on record while I counted down the hours to have these lips again.

Chapter Ten

Hailee

I yawned as Rachel rattled off the customer complaints we'd received last week. Monday mornings at work were always reserved for Rachel's weekly rundown of the week ahead, plus a reflection on the past week. Sadly, her favourite thing seemed to be to berate each of us for our mistakes rather than to build us up by focusing more on our strengths. I was all for acknowledging where we could have done better, but I was a firm believer in motivating through encouragement.

"Are we interrupting your sleep, Hailee?" Rachel threw me a glare as I yawned.

I sat up straighter. "Sorry." God, she irritated me lately. We used to have a great work relationship, but that was back when her love of belittling people hadn't existed. Ever since her hubby left her, it was like she was a whole new person. And not a good one.

"If your side project is keeping you up at night and interfering with my business, you'll need to decide which one you want to keep."

I froze. Where the fuck had that come from? "My project has nothing to do with me yawning, Rachel."

Three months ago, I'd started offering free massages to elderly people who couldn't afford them. It was all done in my own time at night and on weekends. Leona had seen what I was doing and had offered some of her time also, and then other local masseuses had come on board, too. Within two months, I'd grown my group of helpers to twenty, and it had turned into a project where I spent a lot of time managing everyone involved. A local journalist had discovered what we were doing when his mother requested a massage, and he'd written a piece about us for the paper. The past month since that article had been published had been hectic. However, I'd worked hard not to let it interfere with my work.

Rachel continued glaring. "Yes, well I highly doubt that, Hailee. I think your commitment to this business has waned."

Leona groaned next to me, and I kicked her under the table. The last thing she needed was to lose her job or hours because she supported me.

"What are you saying?" I asked. I needed to know if I was in jeopardy of losing my job.

Her eyes bored into mine as she said, "I think you need to reconsider your goals in life and decide if you want to pursue your charity massages or if you'd prefer to focus on building a career here."

My chest squeezed with stress. I couldn't afford to lose my job, but no way in hell was I giving up helping people. I wanted to stand and walk out, telling her she could shove her fucking job, but I bit my tongue. I'd try and string her along until I could find a new job, and then I'd take great delight in telling her what I thought. "Okay," I bit out.

She lifted a brow. "Okay?"

"Okay, I'll reconsider everything." I wanted to scrape that damn brow from her face. She was always arching it, indicating her contempt for us.

"Good," she snapped. Turning to address all the staff, she said, "I hope I can count on your continuing loyalty to this business also." And then she exited the room, leaving me with a sick feeling in the pit of my stomach.

"Fuck, Hailee," Leona said. "What are you going to do?"

I looked at her. “Do you really think that if I was willing to give Tricia up because of this project that I wouldn’t hesitate to give up this job?”

Her lips smooshed together in a sad frown. “Yeah, but we both know that you didn’t walk away from your best friend simply because she gave you an ultimatum and made you choose between her and the project.”

She was right. There was a fuckload more that had gone on in that relationship, but the nail in the coffin had been Tricia’s inability to share me with my new friends and the project that made my heart soar.

I nodded. “That’s true. But honestly, I’m going to look for another job,” I said as everyone in the room hustled around us to leave and get started for the day.

Rachel had put the fear of God into them. I’d seen it on their faces. And I’d wondered how many would stick with me and continue to offer free massages. Out of the fifteen masseuses who worked for her, seven of them donated their time to my project. I figured most of them needed this job more than they needed to help elderly people for free.

Leona stood and looked down at me. “I’ve decided to look for another job, too.”

“Oh, God,” I said, standing with her. “You guys really can’t afford to screw around with finances at the moment, Leona. I won’t accept your help with my project anymore.”

“Pfft,” she muttered. “I’d already decided to start looking. This just cements that decision. And if you think you can keep me away from helping, you’re dreaming. I’m with you on this 100 percent.”

I shook my head as I smiled at her. Leona was a stubborn woman, and I knew there was no way to change her mind.

For a day that had started off so well, it hadn't taken long to turn to shit. And yet, I smiled all the way through the day knowing I'd get to see Devil later.

***

I arrived at Flirt early that night. Much earlier than needed to chat with my bandmates before we started playing. After a shitty day with Rachel constantly on my back, I'd decided to dance some stress off.

"What'll it be tonight, babe?" Doug asked when I rested my arms on his counter.

"Hit me with something strong, please."

"Bad day?"

"The worst. I need a strong drink and then an hour or so dancing, and then I'll be good." Thank goodness Doug heavily discounted my drinks, pretty much to the point of not charging me anything. And then putting what I owed him on a bar tab that he allowed me to pay off whenever I had money.

"You want me to blast your music for you?"

I smiled. Doug always looked after me when I felt the need to dance. I loved the good old Aussie rock that the pub preferred to play, but long ago I'd handed Doug a CD with the kind of rock I liked to dance to. I'd frequented the joint for long enough that the regulars put up with my music every now and then.

"You're good to me, Doug."

He made me a drink and said, "Just looking out for your mental health. And maybe mine. You forget that I've experienced your mood swings over the last two years."

I took the drink as he passed it over. "Yeah, no one needs to experience that." I'd had a few meltdowns over the years, especially over assholes who'd treated me badly. Doug, unfortunately, often copped the brunt of them.

He jerked his chin at me. "Drink up. I'll sort your music out."

I took a gulp of the drink. It tasted fruity and very alcoholic—exactly what I'd asked him for. "What is this?"

"It's a zombie. Lots of rum in that one. Guaranteed to give you some buzz."

I finished the drink and then headed out to the dance floor. Doug had already started playing my music, and a few minutes later, I was dancing, eyes closed, working the tension from my body.

A good hour, maybe more, passed before I decided I'd had enough. A few other girls had joined me on the dance floor, but mostly I'd danced alone, which was the way I preferred it. Getting lost in the beat drowned out the thoughts running through my mind, and I always felt refreshed afterwards. Sweaty, but refreshed.

As I made my way towards the back room where there was a bathroom I could shower in, Devil stepped in front of me. His eyes found mine, and I shivered at the desire I saw there. "I've been thinking about you all fucking day, darlin'. And after watching you dance for the last half hour, I'm not sure I can wait another few hours to have you."

"You've been watching me?" The way that turned me on surprised me. I was a performer, but I never thought of it in the way that people were watching me but rather that they were listening to me. I loved the idea of Devil watching me.

His body moved against mine and I felt his need for me. He slid a hand up my neck, behind my ear and into my hair so that he could grasp my head. Nodding, he said, "I had to restrain myself from dragging you off the dance floor and finding somewhere here I could fuck you."

His words caused an ache between my legs. One that only he could fix. And I needed him to fix it right now. Stepping away from him, I grabbed hold of his hand and led him out the back. We hit the staff room a few moments later, and I attempted to lock the door after I'd closed it behind him, but he dragged me to him before I could.

Lifting me, he pushed me up against the wall. I wrapped my arms and legs around him while he pressed his mouth to mine. He then kissed me like he'd been denied my lips for years.

His kiss consumed me.

Every single part of me.

If I thought dancing cleared my thoughts, Devil kissing me completely wiped them from my mind.

When he came up for air, he dropped his eyes so they could roam my body, and said, "Fuck... your body..." He didn't end his sentence, but rather, ran a hand over my breasts.

I took hold of his face so I could bring his gaze back up to meet mine. "You just want me for my body?"

"I want you for a lot fucking more than that, but right now, all I can think about is getting inside you."

Oh. God.

Devil had a way with words, but he also had a way with delivering those words. His voice could well become my kryptonite. It was deep and rumbly and husky and gravelly all rolled into one. And he knew just when to inflect it with one tone more than the other to achieve his desired goal.

I kept hold of his face and smashed my lips down onto his. He groaned as our tongues tangled in a needy rush. Devil was physically everything in a man I'd ever dreamt of. Besides the muscles and strength he possessed, he exuded the kind of sexuality every woman wanted to experience in their lifetime. Even if he tried to hide his desire for a woman, I was fairly sure he'd struggle, because his entire being revealed it.

It was in the way his chest and hips opened up to me, the way his hands reached for me, the way his mouth fell open even when I was sure he didn't realise, the way his breaths quickened, and the way his eyes glazed over with heat.

I loved the way he didn't try to hide it.

And I loved the feeling of being in the arms of someone who so clearly wanted me.

Devil moved so he could place my feet back on the ground, but his lips stayed glued to mine. When he had me in place, he reached down to lift my dress.

Thank fuck I wore a dress tonight.

I dug my fingernails into the skin at the nape of his neck when his hands found my panties.

I started panting through our kisses when his fingers slid under my panties.

And when two of his fingers easily entered me, I cried out, "Oh, God, yes!"

"Fuck," he groaned into my mouth while he momentarily stopped kissing me. "I fucking love your pussy." Our eyes met and I sucked in a breath. I could listen to Devil talk dirty all night, and if he looked at me the way he was right now, I would do absolutely anything he requested. "I want to finger you for hours, darlin'. I want to make you come over and over by reaching deep inside you and"—he hit my G spot, causing me to cry out with pleasure—"doing that." His mouth was still near mine as he spoke, and the moment he finished talking, he dragged my bottom lip into his mouth and sucked it before kissing me again.

The sound of people talking just outside the door made me remember we hadn't locked it. I pulled my mouth from his. "You need to lock the door."

His eyes dipped to my throat and he bent to kiss me there, sucking hard on my skin. Ignoring my request.

"Devil," I urged, "the door."

Glancing up at me, he shook his head. "I'm going to fuck you with the door unlocked, Hailee."

Fuck.

No.

Any of my bandmates could walk in on us. Or Doug. Or any of the other staff working that night.

I let him go so I could move to lock it myself, but he quickly held me in place. Shaking his head, he growled, "No." Pressing his mouth to my ear, he said, "I'm going to do this"—he reached his fingers deeper in me, adding another as he did so—"until you come, and then I'm going to give you my cock. And the door's going to stay unlocked during all of that."

I wanted that damn door locked.

And yet, I wanted everything he'd just promised me with the door unlocked.

I was torn.

The threat of someone walking in on us caused a whole new level of lust for him.

I wanted him to fuck me hard with his fingers.

I wanted him to fuck me dirty with his dick.

And I wanted him to growl filthy words in my ear while he did all that. *While I worried about someone seeing us.*

I drew his mouth back to mine. "I'm going to let you fuck me with the door unlocked, and in return, you're gonna eat me like you're a starved man later tonight."

His breathing picked up as he bit my lip. "Two things. One, you get no say in the lock. Just so you realise who's in charge here." My legs turned to jelly. I already thought they had, but I was so wrong about that. "And two, I *am* gonna eat you like a starved man later, because I *am* a fucking starved man. I've never known this level of hunger in my life." He kissed me deeply then, messing up any last thought I may have had, before dragging his mouth away to look me in the eyes and say, "Just so you realise how much I want you."

His fingers continued to work their magic inside me while he spoke, and I came as he told me how much he wanted me. I sagged against him as the pleasure consumed me. His strong arms held me up while his lips peppered kisses down my neck to my throat and out along my collarbones.

My need for his cock intensified when his hands roamed my body a moment later. The unlocked door was all but forgotten as I desperately undid his jeans and reached inside them for his cock.

He stopped what he was doing and chuckled. "You want some dick, darlin'?"

"You have no idea, bossman. Now, please tell me, for the love of God, that you have a condom." I was going to scream if he didn't. And I'd possibly hurt him in some way.

His grin spread right across his face as he reached into his back pocket. When he pulled a condom from his wallet, I motioned for him to hurry up and put it on. "Why the hurry?" he asked, taking his sweet time.

I took hold of his chin. "There's gonna be hell to pay if you don't hurry up and get that condom on and fuck me."

The grin on his face grew. Not that I would have thought it possible, but it did.

"What are you grinning at?" I demanded, feeling all kinds of desperate for him to speed this along.

As he slid the condom on, he kissed me and then said, "I'm grinning because I'm thinking that if you can be this demanding for my cock after only knowing me a week, I'm fucking excited to think about how demanding you'll be after a few years."

I reached for his ass to pull him closer in an effort to get him inside me. Circling my arms around him, I lifted myself into his hold as I said, "And what makes you think I'll still be demanding anything from you in a few years?"

He gripped my hair and yanked my head back as he thrust inside of me. Licking a line from my throat up to my mouth, he rasped, "You will be. There's no way you'll ever be able to go without this cock again."

I closed my eyes as he fucked me, and I thought about the truth in that statement. I'd never experienced love at first sight or instant lust in my life. Not until Devil. I'd only had to have one taste to know I wanted to drown in him. I came for the second time as that knowledge sank in.

Devil had wrapped himself around me after only one week, and I didn't ever want to escape.

Chapter Eleven

Devil

"How's Jen?" King asked me early Tuesday morning when he phoned to check in.

"I've just left your place. She seems good today. Better than the last couple of days." She'd perked up a lot since I'd started checking in on her last Friday.

"She still sick?"

"Yeah, that morning sickness is really knocking her around. Nothing seems to be helping too much." She'd been so sick yesterday that I'd googled for suggestions to ease it, but nothing much came up in the results that she hadn't already tried.

"I'm hoping we'll be finished up here in the next day or so. We're heading out to Warwick today and will check in that area for Shannon. Scott got a lead for us out there." He paused for a moment before asking, "How's Hyde? Is his head in the game?"

Fuck, Hyde had been off the grid most of the time since King left on Friday. He'd shown his face for an hour or so yesterday, but that was it. I didn't want to burden King while he was away, but he'd made it clear he wanted to know this kind of shit. "I've hardly seen him, King, so I can't really answer that. I've left a message for him to make sure he's at the drop this afternoon, but I'm yet to hear back." We had a shipment of coke coming in at four, and I needed Hyde with me for it. The motherfuckers who supplied us had grown increasingly hostile lately. Fuck knew what I'd do if he didn't show.

"Fuck," King muttered. "I'll call him, too. Let me know if you don't hear back from him in the next hour or so."

After we ended the call, I placed my phone on the counter of the bar where I sat in the clubhouse and found Kree watching me with concern. "What?" I asked her. She'd grown into a good friend the past few months, and I often ran shit by her because she always came up with good suggestions.

She leant her hip against the counter. "Is Hyde okay?"

I shrugged. "I don't know. Why?"

"He doesn't seem okay to me. Working in the bar, I hear a lot of whispers. And it seems to me that you're all frustrated with him, but it also seems that no one has checked on him."

"Fuck, Kree, you know what Hyde's like. He doesn't let anyone in. I've tried to talk with him a few times, but he either shuts down or loses his shit with me. There're only so many times someone can be told to fuck off before they do. What do you expect me to do if he's not interested in sharing whatever is on his mind?"

"Ask again. And again. Devil, friends don't give up on each other. Eventually he'll confide in someone, but only if he knows you care."

I sat and contemplated what she said while she poured drinks for some of the guys. She was right. But, Hyde could be a prick. Knowing that, though, told me I was the club member who would have to try harder to get through to him. Fuck knew, none of the others would have the patience.

***

"Since when did you start smoking again?" I asked Hyde while we waited for the drop that afternoon. Thank fuck he'd turned up. Not that he'd bothered to reply to my message or King's.

He glared at me. "None of your fucking business."

Hyde had quit smoking two years earlier. He'd always been a heavy smoker, so it had stunned all of us when he'd just up and quit one day. After the way he stopped cold turkey, I'd never expected him to take it back up.

"Why the fuck are you such an asshole, Hyde? I don't get it. We're your brothers, just trying to look out for you, and you treat us like absolute fucking shit some days." None of us knew much about his past, and that seemed to be the way he preferred it. I'd never pushed to know more, because I believed everyone had a right to privacy, but maybe knowing more about him would help me understand why he was the way he was.

He took a long drag on his smoke as he stared into the distance. We were waiting outside an abandoned warehouse that we used as one of our drop-off points. Thunder rumbled overhead, and the clouds darkened, threatening for the sky to open and dump rain on us. Hyde's features darkened, too, as he contemplated my question.

Finally, he looked at me and said, "You ever done something that altered your entire life, Devil? Something that also impacted other people's lives, too. In a bad way, I mean."

I thought about that for a moment. The answer wasn't one I wanted to think about too much. "I've done bad shit that's affected other people's lives. And it affected me, too, but I wouldn't say it altered my life entirely. Why?"

"I have."

"And?" I wasn't sure where he was going with this.

He finished his smoke and stubbed it out before glancing back up at me. "And… I think maybe I fucked up more than I thought I did."

Kree was so fucking right. Hyde needed us. As I tried to figure out how to word what I wanted to say, the guys we were waiting for showed up, and the moment was lost.

I watched as Hyde stalked their way, his body tense, and I hoped like hell this drop went okay. His unpredictable nature concerned me, so I hurried to catch up to him.

Rolland had brought three guys with him today instead of the one he usually showed up with. We'd agreed a year ago when we started working together that we'd both only ever bring one person with us to these drops.

"What's going on?" I asked him when we met in the middle. I jerked my chin towards the men he'd brought. "What happened to the deal we had?"

His shifty eyes moved between Hyde and me. He knew us both because King always switched up who he brought with him. "Got shit to discuss with you boys today and didn't wanna take a chance that the information I'm about to share would get me killed."

"Fuck," Hyde said. "Start talking and let's see how this shakes out."

Sweat rolled down Rolland's face, and I figured it wasn't just because of the heat. A large thunderclap overhead caused him to jump. "Fuck," he muttered. "This shit ain't all on me, so you just keep that in mind, yeah?"

I stepped forward. "When Hyde tells you to start talking, he doesn't mean to start talking shit. Spit it the fuck out!"

He raked his fingers through his hair. "Okay, so the deal for me to only supply Storm... it has to end." As he said that, the three men with him all pulled their guns and trained them on us. "As of today, I'll be supplying you and one other guy. And like I said, this ain't my preferred decision. I owe someone."

Hyde's lips pulled up into a snarl. "Who else are you supplying?"

"He's a new player in town. I doubt you know him."

Hyde grasped Rolland's shirt, ignoring that two guns were instantly trained on him. "I didn't fucking ask if I know him, motherfucker. I asked you for his name."

The biggest guy that Rolland had brought with him pressed his gun to Hyde's head. "I suggest you back the fuck away, asshole. I'm under strict instructions to shoot if you threaten any of us today."

Hyde ignored him and continued to stare at Rolland. "I'm waiting!" he barked.

"Rolland," I started, but the big guy turned his gun on me, causing me to stop.

"Oh for fuck's sake," Rolland muttered. "You're gonna find out anyway. I owe loyalty to no fucker. His name is Wesley Marx." He paused for a moment before saying, "Now, can we get this shit done so we can all leave?"

The last thing I wanted to do was carry on as if nothing had happened. Wesley Marx cutting in on our territory was a big fucking deal, and King would probably hunt him down and threaten to slit his throat if he didn't stop. But with three guns on us, Hyde and I didn't have much choice but to carry on.

As we watched Rolland leave after we'd completed the drop, I said to Hyde, "This is gonna get messy."

He glanced at me and nodded. "I'll look into who Wesley Marx is and you let King know about all this."

"You don't want to let King know?" He was the VP after all.

"No, you do it."

I narrowed my eyes at him. "You wanna finish that story you were telling me earlier?" Whatever it was, I felt like it must tie in with the shit going down between him and King.

His eyes turned hard. "No. And don't bring that shit up again." With that, he turned and stalked to the van we'd brought to the drop. And I wondered if that would be my only chance to get Hyde to open up.

***

Just after five thirty, I pulled up outside Hailee's work. When I dropped her at home that morning after she stayed the night at my place again, I'd told her I'd pick her up. She was a stubborn woman and argued with me, sprouting some bullshit about being capable of walking. I'd given her a good five minutes in which to argue with me, and then I'd told her how this would go. She'd argued for another five minutes before finally giving in. I figured that was ten minutes well spent, because I planned to pick her up every day from here on out.

"You're late," she said, walking my way. She'd been perched on the low brick wall outside her work, waiting for me.

I remained on my bike and passed her a helmet. "How long you been waiting, darlin'?"

"Maybe like five to ten minutes. Somewhere in that range."

I grinned. "Bullshit. I just did the block trying to find somewhere to park. You weren't waiting out here then."

She poked her tongue at me, a cheeky smile pushing its way through. "I've gotta keep you on your toes somehow. Start as you wish to go on, and all."

I reached for her waist and pulled her close before she had a chance to put the helmet on. "For the record, I'm on my toes. But I do like your style."

"Good to hear," she said as she hopped on the bike behind me.

Reaching back for her, I grabbed her thighs and slid her along the bike towards me. "You're too far away. I need that sweet pussy against my ass."

She did as I said and wrapped her arms tightly around my waist. It occurred to me a moment too late that by the time we made it to her place, my dick would be like steel. Not the best way to turn up for dinner with her grandmother.

For the next forty minutes, we weaved in and out of some of the worst Sydney traffic I'd seen in a long time. This meant that when we arrived at Hailee's home, my prediction had proved correct.

Hailee's eyes travelled from my crotch to meet my gaze as we stood in her driveway. She didn't say anything, but the way her lips twitched gave me an idea of her thoughts.

"You're amused by my pain?" I asked.

She frowned. "It hurts?"

"No, but *I'm* in pain. One, I really don't wanna go inside to your grandmother like this. And two, I'm pained that I have to wait to get you under me. I'm all for dinner and talking with Jean, but a man should be able to pick his woman up from work and take her straight home to bed."

Her face and body softened in a way that caused *me* to soften. The woman who had told me she wanted to keep me on my toes was all but gone, replaced by a woman who looked at me like I'd made all the bad in her day disappear just by being there.

She swayed a little as she clutched a handful of my shirt. "Your woman? We've only known each other for just over a week."

My eyes searched hers. "You don't believe that two people can meet and just *know* they're meant to be together?"

"I don't know.... I've never put much thought into that. I guess I've never met a man who fit that category." Her words stumbled out in much the same way I figured her thoughts were stumbling all over each other. I'd caught her off guard, and it was a fucking beautiful place to catch her.

From what I knew so far, Hailee wasn't a closed off person, but when she was open like this, she was even more beautiful than usual.

It all affected me. The way she chewed on her lip, and the way her thoughts caused her to waver between being a little lost and being completely there with me. Also, the way she smiled at me like I really was the only person in the world. And how she gave me her complete attention. She made me feel like whatever I had to say was important enough for her to consider.

Hailee had this kind of gentle yet spirited soul I'd never known in a woman before. Not that I knew her that well yet, but even if she tried to hide from the world, she'd never be able to. Her inner beauty shone just as brightly as her outer beauty.

"You've never met a man who fit that category because *I'm* that man for you."

She processed that for a beat. "I don't know that I believe in knowing someone is the person for you straight away. I thought the last guy I was in a long-term relationship with was the one for me. Turned out that after two years of living with him, I didn't know him at all. And instead of giving me a lifetime of happiness, all he gave me was self-doubt and a fear of falling for the wrong man again."

Her gaze had drifted to the ground as she spoke, and my gut told me this asshole had fucked her right up. Tilting her chin up, I said, "What did he do to you?"

Her eyes met mine and she swallowed hard. "I don't really want to talk about this tonight," she said in a half whisper.

I moved closer to her. "Hailee, what did he do?"

She blinked a few times and her body stilled. I wasn't convinced she was going to give me what I wanted, but then she opened her mouth and shared a piece of her soul with me. One of the many pieces I'd be fighting to own from here on out. "He started to change just after we'd been together for two years. Like, he'd lose his shit if I came home from work late, or he'd pick a fight with me after dinner and then go out for the entire night, not coming home until the morning and refusing to tell me where he'd been. His moods swung all the time until the point where I didn't know what to expect from one hour to the next. He would go from him telling me how much he loved me to him belittling me and telling me I didn't deserve anyone in my life and that I should be lucky he chose to stay with me. It got to the point where I decided we needed a break. I wasn't sure if I was going to leave him all together, but I did need some time away from him to think straight." She paused for a moment and took a few deep breaths before continuing. "That day… the day I told him I needed some time away… he beat me so badly I couldn't go to work for a week."

"Motherfucker," I swore. Pulling her into my arms, I kissed her head and said, "Men like that don't deserve to breathe."

She clung to me for a while. When she pulled away, she said, "No, they don't."

"You left him after that?"

She nodded. "I called my brother for help. I was living in the UK at the time and had no money to fly home. He flew to me, sorted Mickey out and then brought me home. And while I'll always be grateful for what he did for me, he's been a pain in my ass ever since. He's so damn overprotective now when it comes to men I date that he scares most of them off."

"I like him already. That's exactly what I'd hope a brother would do for you."

She raised a brow. "Yeah, you wait until you meet him and then tell me what you think. I bet you'll agree with me soon enough."

"Okay, so let's get one thing clear here. You're my woman."

She smiled. "Is that your way of telling me you don't want me to see anyone else?"

"It is. It's also my way of telling you that from here on out, I'll be picking you up from work every day and dropping you off, too." I placed a finger against her lips when she attempted to argue with me. "And that Sundays are to be reserved for me. I don't care what we do so long as we do it together."

Her eyes widened. "Umm, no, that's not gonna happen, bossman."

"Which part of that?" I had to work hard not to grin at her reaction. I fucking loved going head-to-head with her.

"All of it."

"Uh, yeah, it is."

"No." She shook her head emphatically. "There's no way a guy I've just met is gonna tell me what I can and can't do."

"So you're saying that after we've known each other for some time, you'll allow it?"

Her forehead scrunched her disapproval of everything I was saying. "Don't try and twist my words."

I grinned. "Okay, try and word it again. At which point in our relationship do you think it'd be acceptable for me to demand a few things?"

"Never!" Fuck, I was working her up. And in turn, she was working my dick up more than she already had on the way over here.

"Right, I'm glad we've got that settled," I said as I moved towards her house.

She grabbed hold of my arm. "Wait. We haven't settled anything."

I halted my progress and looked at her. "We have. We've worked out that you're gonna fight me all the way, which for the record, I'm already getting hard about." Dipping my mouth to her ear, I added, “I’m not the type of man to give up when I want something, Hailee. And I just told you how much I want you. So fight all you want, but this relationship *is* going to happen, and I *am* going to demand things from you.”

Chapter Twelve

Hailee

I watched Devil laugh as my grandmother told him something funny. He had the most infectious laugh I'd ever heard, and my lips curled up into a smile simply from the sound.

After his declaration outside when we'd arrived, the one where he tried to lay down the law with me about having his way with bossing me around, we'd come inside to find Jean struggling to pull the roast from the oven. Devil had quickly taken over and had also settled my grandmother at the kitchen table with a drink of water. That had earnt him brownie points. And then I'd all but forgotten being mildly irritated with him when he proceeded to finish cooking dinner.

Who knew bikers could cook? Not me. But it had been confirmed when I took my first bite of the honeyed carrots he'd made. I mean, what biker even knew to honey carrots?

"Hailee, cat got your tongue, dear?"

I stared at my grandmother who'd just asked that question, breaking into my thoughts. "Sorry, I was just thinking about something."

"What?" Gran always did ask the hard questions. Well, not hard so much as intrusive.

I decided to share my thoughts. Glancing at Devil, I said, "Who taught you to cook? Specifically, who told you that honey and carrots go so well together?" Looking back at my grandmother, I said, "That's what I was thinking."

Devil grinned. Always with the sexy grin that caused my brain to go fuzzy. "My mother and my sister." He winked as he added, "*Specifically*, it was Lee who taught me about carrots and honey." That wink shot heat straight to my core. God, how I wanted to rip those clothes off him and—

"Lee's your sister?" My grandmother asked, cutting into my dirty thoughts.

"Yeah. She's a year younger than me but was the kind of kid who hounded Mum to let her help cook from the age of three. Mum got pneumonia when I was thirteen, and Lee took over the family cooking. Part of that was roping me and my brother in to help."

"You're close to your sister, then?" Gran asked.

Devil nodded. "Yes, ma'am." He pulled out his wallet and flashed a photo at her. "That's Lee's daughter, Skye. She's just turned one." I wasn't sure I'd ever seen a man beam so much while talking about his family. And yet, I knew from a previous conversation that he hadn't seen his parents for fifteen years, so I wondered what his family looked like these days.

I leant forward. "Do you see them often?"

Regret clouded his features as he shook his head. "No. Lee and her husband settled in Tamworth where we grew up. I haven't been back there since I left home, so the only time I see them is when Lee comes to Sydney. And that's probably only once a year. But we Skype, so Skye knows who I am."

Silence fell over us for a moment. I didn't know what to say, because he appeared sad about not seeing them often. And that was an emotion I was yet to meet in Devil, so it required a moment of thought on my behalf as to how to approach it.

My grandmother, though, jumped right on it, changing the subject completely. "Hailee tells me she doesn't know your real name, young man. Is that correct?"

Oh. God.

"Gran," I chastised her, hitting her with a dirty look.

She gave me the look she reserved for when she intended to ignore my plea. “Hush, Hailee. If a man wants to see my granddaughter, he’d better be offering up his name. I need to know who has my baby out at night in case anything happens.”

And there it was.

Jean Archer showed her love in cantankerous ways that I both adored her for and argued with her over. She was just like Aaron—she’d never stopped worrying about me since I arrived home from England.

Devil’s face turned serious, and I knew that he knew where she was coming from, too. He nodded. “My name is Dominic Ford.”

Dominic.

His name sat on the tip of my tongue. It totally suited him.

“Thank you, Dominic,” Gran said as she stood. “I’ll be right back.”

Watching her hobble out of the room, he frowned. “Is she okay?”

I sprinkled some salt onto my veggies. “She’s starting to have some health problems and has fallen a couple of times lately, but mostly she’s doing great.”

Looking up from my dinner, I caught the thoughtful expression on his face. Warmth flooded my belly that he not only seemed genuinely worried about a woman he’d only recently met, but that he’d also taken the time to help her, answer her questions and begin getting to know her. Not one other man I’d dated had ever done that. Sure, they’d feigned interest in her, but to them, she was just an old lady who was part of the package with me.

“She needs a railing put on those front steps,” he said, “And does she have a rail in the shower? I can organise that too if you need it.”

"Wait. What?" I'd been deep in thought and was sure I must have missed something he'd said. "Did you just say you'd install some railings?"

"Yeah, I'll get some of the boys to help me. We can probably swing by in a couple of days and do it."

I held up my hand to stop him talking. "Devil, you don't need to do that. And besides, I'd have to clear it with the landlord first."

"Who's your real estate?"

I stared at him in silence while I contemplated everything he'd just said. "You're going to take charge of this, aren't you? If I tell you the name of the real estate, you'll just go and sort it out with them?"

"Hailee, your grandmother is unsteady on her legs. She needs help, and I can give it to her," he said as if he thought he had to defend his choice. Which he didn't.

Still staring at him, I smiled. Huge. And my heart burst open a little more. He had no idea what he'd just done. Standing, I moved to where he sat and kissed him. Long and hard. When we came up for air, I said, "Thank you."

He reached for my hand and held me in place before I could move back to my chair. "I feel like you're thanking me for a whole lot more than a couple of railings," he murmured, his eyes holding a question.

I slowly nodded and folded myself into his lap, my arms looped around his neck. "My grandfather screwed around on my grandmother and left her when I was only young. Her daddy had left all his money to my grandfather, thinking he'd look after her forever. But when he left her, he took everything. She had to move in with us just so she could afford to live. When he died, he left his money to my father, and I thought she'd be okay after that." I took a breath before continuing. "However, when Dad passed away, Mum got everything. I'm pretty sure he assumed she would continue to look after his mother, but Mum treated her awfully. Mum gives me a small amount of money each month to care for Gran, but it's nowhere near enough. I'm drowning in bills, and every day I wake up not knowing how I'm going to care for my grandmother as she gets older. I also don't have a lot of spare time to organise stuff like this. You offering what you have is a huge load off my mind." My voice choked on that last sentence, because even though I'd said he'd taken a huge load off my mind, that didn't even begin to cover it.

I knew that for a man to offer this at the beginning of a relationship meant that there'd be more like this to come. And that right there caused my emotions to jump all over the place.

Before Devil could reply, my grandmother joined us again. Taking her seat at the table, she said, "The man's a keeper, Hailee."

Devil's smiled, but he didn't say anything. Didn't offer a cheeky reply. He simply kept quiet and waited for me to speak. The space I'd started to clear for him in my heart grew a little. I liked that he seemed to understand my emotional response to what he'd offered. That he understood my need for a moment to get my thoughts under control.

I pressed my lips to his again for a brief moment. "I'm beginning to think he is, too," I said softly when I ended the kiss.

As I moved back to my seat, Gran said to Devil, "We use that little real estate on the corner near the pub."

"The one near the meditation studio. And it's Brett who we deal with there," I threw in.

"I'll contact them tomorrow," he said.

My grandmother engaged him in a conversation about gardening after that. Time in the garden was one of her loves, and she would talk anyone's ear off if they gave her the space to do it. Devil gave her that space, and while I listened in for the first few moments, I quickly drifted away to thoughts of him and all the things I didn't know about him yet. I couldn't wait to get to know everything.

Chapter Thirteen

Devil

I eyed Hailee apologetically as we stood in her hallway. "I'm sorry, darlin', but I've gotta go."

We'd finished dinner just over an hour earlier and had been watching television with Jean since then. Well, Jean had been watching television; Hailee and I had been fighting to keep our hands to ourselves while her grandmother was in the room with us.

"It's all good. You should go and help your friend out," Hailee said.

Nitro had called to ask me if I could head over to Monroe's place and check on her. He'd received a garbled message from Tatum about something to do with Monroe and couldn't get hold of her to find out what it was.

My phone buzzed with a text.

Nitro: Take Hyde with you. Just heard from Tatum. There's some asshole threatening Monroe.

Me: Is Tatum there too?

Nitro: No, thank fuck. Although she'd probably take the guy down given half a chance.

Me: True. Hyde's on his way. I already phoned him.

Nitro: Let me know when you're done.

I slid my arm around Hailee's waist and kissed her. "Thanks for dinner. I'll text you when I'm done and see if you're still awake." I didn't think she would be because she'd yawned her way through the TV show.

"Okay," she said, but as I moved to leave, she grabbed a handful of my shirt and held me in place. "Be safe." I heard the concern in her voice.

"There's nothing to worry about. Nitro's just overprotective." I wasn't sure, though. Nitro might have been extremely protective of Tatum and Monroe, but he wasn't the type to worry easily. However, I wanted to put Hailee's mind at ease.

She let me go and said, "I'll talk to you later. And, Devil… thank you for humouring my grandmother and watching television with her."

I smoothed her hair back off her face. Fuck, she had no idea how far gone I was. "Hailee, I want to know every little thing about you, and part of that is your family. I'd have gone to Mars with Jean if that's what she wanted."

Her eyes lit up, and I knew I'd said the right thing. I hadn't been stretching the truth, though. Not that lying was my thing with women, but I'd been known to smooth the truth over a little in my time. With Hailee, I didn't want to chance fucking this up.

She shooed me away with the flick of her wrists. "Go, before I beg you to stay."

On the way to Monroe's place, it struck me how different Hailee was to all the other women I'd dated. She hadn't sulked or tried to stop me from leaving. There was none of the guilt trips I was used to from women. And she'd been more concerned for me than she'd been disappointed I had to leave. It was a fucking refreshing change.

***

Hyde was already at Monroe's by the time I arrived.

"Just got here about two minutes ago, brother," he said. "You hear anything else from Nitro?"

I nodded. "Yeah, apparently someone was threatening her."

"Okay, you want me to take the back?"

"Sounds good."

Hyde headed around to find the back door while I investigated the front. I couldn't hear any yelling or arguing and all seemed to be okay. So, I knocked on the door and waited to see if Monroe answered.

She did, after she checked me out through the curtain and unlocked a bunch of locks on her front door.

"Thanks for coming, but the guy's gone. He did, however, do something I think you might be interested in seeing and hearing about," she said as she motioned for me to enter.

I stepped inside her tiny home. It was one of those brick boxes that probably only had two bedrooms and not much living space. But, she'd made it homely, and I found myself drawn to the framed photographs lining her walls. That, and the crazy wallpaper. I wasn't sure, but I could have sworn I saw cats on the wallpaper in her lounge room as we passed it.

She led me into her very retro kitchen. Between the aqua coloured stove and fridge, to the red-and-white chequered floor, to the zany, weird multicoloured ornaments she'd filled the room with, I didn't know where to look first. Not until a guy came into view. And then all my attention zeroed in on him.

Before I could say anything, Hyde entered the kitchen, too. My gaze met his. "You pick the lock or break the door?"

"Fuck," Monroe muttered, looking at Hyde. "Tell me you didn't break my door."

Hyde stilled for a moment in a way I'd never seen him still. His eyes ran all over her. He took so long to answer her that I cut into whatever thoughts were running through his mind.

"Hyde. You break the door, brother?"

His gaze snapped to mine. "No." Glancing back at Monroe, he said, "Your door is in one piece."

Relief filled her features. "Thank fuck. That'd be an expense I could do without at the moment."

I eyed the guy sitting at her kitchen table. Jerking my chin at him, I said, "What happened?"

Before he could reply, Monroe jumped in. "This is what that asshole did. Fox drove me home from work and stayed for dinner. The asshole must have followed us from work. We'd just finished when the guy knocks on the front door and barges his way in when I open it. He looked so damn friendly when I checked who it was in the window. And he held up one of those—" She snapped her fingers as she searched for the word.

Fox volunteered the information when she couldn't. "He had religious shit with him."

"Yes!" Monroe explained. "That's the only reason I opened the door at this time of night. I wanted to say thanks but fuck off. In a nice way, of course. I mean, those guys are only trying to help the world, right? But I've got no need for religion in my life."

Hyde stood staring at Monroe in silence. I could never get a good read on him, but he appeared a little bewildered by her. Understandable, though, because she was always like a wild rush of energy every time I saw her. He'd never met her. Not that I knew of, so I guessed he was still getting his bearings with her.

Turning back to Fox, I said, "Okay, so why the fuck did he cut your face up like that?" Fox's face was a nasty mess of cuts and blood. By the looks of the first aid box on the table, Monroe had been attempting to clean him up, but he was still a mess.

"I owe a guy for some coke."

"And?" I said.

"And he sent the motherfucker around to collect."

I frowned. "Monroe, I'm not sure how this is of interest to us."

"Well," she started, "the guy said that we should remember his boss's name—Wesley Marx—because he was about to become the main supplier in Sydney. And that Storm didn't know what was about to hit them."

Wesley fucking Marx. The asshole who was using our supplier.

"Why would he mention us?" Hyde finally joined the conversation.

Monroe glanced at him. "I told him he should be more careful about who he threatens, because I have Storm on speed dial. That's when he mentioned your club. He seemed pissed off that I even mentioned you."

"Really?" I said. "Storm on speed dial?" I tried not to laugh. I had no idea where women came up with some shit.

She waved her hands in the air dismissively. "Well, I've got Nitro. By default. That counts, right?"

Hyde's lips twitched in amusement. Fuck, I'd never seen that in my life. The only emotions I knew from him were anger or begrudging acceptance. "Yeah, sugar, that counts."

Sugar?

Jesus.

Monroe hit him with a smile that could have blasted light to Antarctica. I watched in fascination as her entire body language switched from alert to soft. She'd come a long way since I'd met her when Nitro first took up with Tatum. Monroe had been wary with me at first. Trusting a biker, she told me, was like trusting a teenage boy with your virginity—you hoped for the best, but would most likely end up fucked over and wishing you'd not put your faith in them. And after all that, there she was looking at Hyde like he was the only other person in this room.

I took charge. "Okay, so if you're okay and don't need us, I'm gonna report this back to Nitro and then go finish what I was doing before he called."

Monroe nodded her agreement. Staring at Hyde, she said, "Thanks for coming. I'll let you boys know if we see that asshole again."

As I was about to leave, something struck me. Turning back to Fox, I said, "This guy? You ever seen him before?"

Fox shook his head. "Nope."

"You been buying off Marx for long?"

"I've never met Marx. The dude I buy from is a scrawny teenager I met when his brother came to get a tattoo."

"So he works for Marx, too?"

"Yeah, but I don't know how Marx is about to become so big in Sydney when he's only ever been some two-bit operation."

"Thanks for the info, man," I said.

As we exited Monroe's home, I said to Hyde, "Seems to me that someone is backing Marx. And we need to find out who that is."

Chapter Fourteen

Hailee

I drank half the martini Devil bought me before stopping and placing the glass on the table we sat at in the busy Italian restaurant he'd brought me to for dinner. "It was a long shitty day."

And a long crappy week. Work used to be my happy place. Not so much anymore. Thank God for Friday.

The thing that had kept me going during the days was the time I spent with Devil at night. He made good on his promise to pick me up after work every day, and I looked forward to that each day. Not to mention the long nights of sex. After locking us away at his house for a couple of nights, though, he'd insisted we go out for dinner that night.

"Any luck finding jobs to apply for?" I'd told him how and why Rachel was being a bitch, and he had encouraged me to search for a new job.

I shrugged. "I've found a couple, but none of them really excite me. Plus, none are as close to home as Rachel's."

"How was she today?"

I rolled my eyes. "She was still going on about me needing to work out my priorities. If I have to sit through another week of that next week, I may just stab her in the eye with a pointy stick. I mean, I've worked for her for two years and never once given her any reason to treat my badly. I've tried pointing out that the free massages don't hurt her business, but she seems to have it in for my project." I drank some more of my cocktail and added, "I just don't get it."

"Have any more of your volunteers pulled out?"

I nodded. "Yeah, I've lost four in total now. So I had to spend my lunch hour reworking the schedule for the next week. I think I've got it sorted. So long as no more leave me. It just means that I'm going to be busy a few nights next week and all day next Saturday doing massages."

He grinned. "I tell you what, darlin', I'll massage your tired body afterwards."

I couldn't help but smile. Devil had a knack for making me laugh when I didn't think it possible. He'd made this week bearable. "Let me guess, you'll pay special attention to certain parts of my tired, weary body... like, my feet and hands."

His grin broadened. "Definitely your hands. We don't need them to get too sore and tired. I have plans for those hands."

"And do I need to pay you for these massages? Or are you doing it from the goodness of your heart?"

"I do everything from the goodness of my heart, but a blow job wouldn't be a bad form of payment."

My body relaxed as all the tension Rachel had caused seeped away. I lifted my glass to my mouth and said, "If you play your cards right, you may just score one of those tonight."

I drank the last of my cocktail after that, enjoying the way he responded to what I'd said. Just watching Devil was something I could spend all my time doing, but watching him while pleasure and satisfaction danced across his face took my enjoyment to a whole new level.

It was while we sat in silence simply gazing at each other that my brother slid into the booth next to me, joining us.

"Aaron, uh, what are you doing here?" I faltered on my words because he'd caught me by surprise.

He gave me a tight smile. Glancing back and forth between Devil and me, he said, "I'm here for dinner with a friend and just happened to see you as the waiter took us to our table. Figured I'd come and say hi to my little sister and see what she's up to since I haven't heard from her for a week." He zeroed in on Devil when he added, "*And* since she never told me she'd started dating a new guy."

His gaze met Devil's as he said that, and I didn't miss the look that passed between them. I wasn't sure what it meant, but I guessed it was some male thing that we women would never understand. I suspected Aaron's eyes were saying, "Don't fuck with my sister or I'll slice your dick off before I feed you to the sharks," while Devil's eyes said, "We're cool, man, no need to threaten death to my dick."

"Since when do I have to report in with you every time I go out with a man?" His attitude annoyed me. It seemed to be way worse than ever before, too. I figured that maybe they knew each other, but wasn't sure. I never had spoken to Devil about that day in the back of Aaron's car. We'd had other things on our minds.

Aaron didn't respond to that, but rather, said, "You two meet that day at the animal protest and then just decide to start seeing each other?"

Devil ignored the attitude blazing from Aaron. "No, man. We met again after that at the pub Hailee's band plays at."

"How long do you intend to date Hailee?" Aaron's voice took that hard edge he often reserved for when he was working. I hated that he used it on Devil.

Devil didn't appear surprised in the least that Aaron was being an asshole. "For as long as she'll have me."

Aaron's body tensed next to me. He was built, so we were crammed into my side of the booth, sides touching, and I felt his turn rock hard. "I don't see it going anywhere."

I spun sideways to face him. "Aaron!" I chastised. "Do you mind? How dare you come here and be so damn rude."

He hardly even acknowledged me. Instead, he kept his focus completely on Devil and said, "Hailee's been through enough shit with men to last her a lifetime. She sure as fuck doesn't need you coming along and breaking her heart when you decide to show her who you really are." Anger was practically rolling off him, and I couldn't figure out where it came from.

"Right, I think that's enough," I snapped. "You need to leave."

Devil cut in with a shake of his head. "Darlin', why don't you give your brother and me a moment to have a chat?"

"Really? You wanna sit here and listen to more of that?"

"Yeah, I do."

I stared at him, wondering what he thought he could achieve with Aaron. It was then that I decided he didn't know Aaron at all, because if he did, he'd know there was no talking my brother around when he'd made up his mind.

"Okay," I said. "Good luck."

Aaron let me out of the booth, and I left them to it. I headed to the ladies room to freshen up and prayed like hell they didn't take each other's heads off.

Chapter Fifteen

Devil

If Bronze thought I would give Hailee up, he was seriously mistaken. As we sat watching each other, his eyes full of mistrust, mine with determination, I knew I was in for a hell of a fight.

He rested his arms on the table and leant forward, his nostrils flaring. "Get the fuck up and walk the fuck out of this restaurant now."

My hands clenched by my side. Because he was Hailee's brother and a club ally, I gave him the space to be an asshole. "Bronze—"

He cut me off without hearing a word I planned to say. "I don't want to hear it, Devil."

"And what the fuck did you think I was about to say?"

"Some bullshit about how you don't plan to hurt her, or how you're different to other guys, or some other fucking lie about how much you care about her. I've heard it all before from the other motherfuckers she's dated, and I've seen the proof of it being nothing but bull." He leant forward even more. "Tell me, Devil, you have a sister?"

"I do. And—"

"And you ever had to fly across the fucking world to save her from a man who wanted to beat her until she agreed to stay with him? You ever seen your sister's face so bruised and swollen you hardly recognised her?"

"No." I knew better by that point to just answer his question and let him continue. He'd only cut me off if I tried to get a word in.

"Yeah, well let me tell you, it's something I never plan to do or see again." He took a breath. His chest was pumping up and down rapidly as he worked himself up. "The last fucking thing Hailee needs is to get mixed up with Storm. I know the kind of men your club deals with, and like fuck will I sit back and watch my sister get involved with something or someone who could bring harm her way. You get me?"

I met his gaze as I rested my arms on the table, too. "I get you, Bronze. Completely. But there's no way in hell I'd allow any harm to come to Hailee. It'd be over my dead fucking body."

He stood. "I'm not interested in hearing it. I'm telling you now, walk the fuck away from my sister."

As he took a few steps away, I called out, "I'm not leaving her, Bronze."

He stopped and turned back to face me. Steam practically billowed out of his head. "I'm warning you, Devil. The consequences of you not doing what I've asked won't be pretty." Without another word exchanged, he stalked to his table.

I stared after him, pissed off. He could threaten me all he liked, but no fucking way would I walk away from his sister. Not unless she told me to. And even then, she'd have a fucking fight on her hands. I wasn't a man who gave up easily. I'd been a fighter since I was a kid, my dad had made sure of that, and I wasn't changing that anytime soon.

***

Just over an hour later, we arrived at King's home after I received a call from Jen towards the end of dinner. She'd been distraught and rambling on about Shannon. I couldn't make sense of what she said so I told her to calm down and I'd come over on my way home.

"I'll just wait out here," Hailee said when we pulled up outside King's place.

"Like fuck you will. I'm not having you standing out here in the dark on your own at this time of night."

Her hand curled around my neck and she pulled me close so she could kiss me. "This protective side of yours gets me so damn excited, bossman. I hope this doesn't take too long because I really need you to get me naked."

I groaned and slapped her ass. "This better not take long. Jen's been highly fucking emotional this week while King's been away, so she probably just needs someone to tell her everything's gonna work out. Shouldn't take too long."

Hailee frowned. "Is something wrong with her?"

I hadn't told her anything about Jen, and wouldn't share much. That was Jen's and King's story to tell. "She's been sick while he's been away. I've been checking in on her, making sure she's doing okay."

Her frown shifted to a smile. "You're a good guy, Devil."

I wavered between wanting to let her keep thinking that and telling her she was far off base. In the end, I went with, "Okay, let's do this so I can get you back to my place and get inside you."

I led the way to the front door, surprised to hear King's voice inside as we approached. I knew he was on his way back to Sydney, but wasn't aware he'd arrived.

"Fuck," I muttered as I made out what was being said. They were arguing over Shannon. I hesitated to knock on the door, not wanting to interrupt them, but when Jen screeched out something about knowing King would never change, and him retaliating with rage, I decided they might need me. Even if only to give King a moment to blow off some steam. I hadn't heard that level of anger from him in a long time and wondered what the hell had inspired it.

Lifting my knuckles to the door, I knocked loud enough to be heard over their shouts. A couple of moments later, King yanked the door open, his wild eyes meeting mine. I sucked in a sharp breath at the madness I saw in him. Not only had his anger come out to play that night, so had his crazy.

Fuck.

The hair on the back of my neck stood up and apprehension prickled over my skin.

I shouldn't have brought Hailee here.

"Devil," King barked, his attention solely on me. It didn't appear that he'd even noticed Hailee standing behind me. "What are you doing here?"

I'd never faltered around King. Had never felt the fear of him that so many did. However, I did in that moment. Not for me, but for Hailee. I couldn't put my finger on the reason, because I didn't believe he'd hurt her, but the need to protect her from him nevertheless churned deep in my gut.

"Jen called me. She seemed upset and confused, so I told her I'd come over. I didn't realise you were home."

"I called him when you took off," Jen said, coming into view behind King. Her tear-stained face was painted with mascara streaks and puffiness. But as much as he'd upset her, the old Jen I'd known seemed to have made an appearance again. I hadn't had a glimpse of her all week when I'd visited. She'd been soft and welcoming, seemingly happy to have my help. The Jen standing in front of me now had the hard glint in her eyes and the don't-fuck-with-me stance that I associated with her from years ago.

King's chest rose and he held his breath for a beat, as if he was working hard not to lose his shit with her. When he finally exhaled a long breath, he said, "Come in, we've got shit to discuss anyway." Stepping aside, he motioned for me to enter.

I hesitated for a split second. King never missed anything and didn't miss this. And he was as fucking perceptive as he always was when he said, "For fuck's sake, Devil, bring her in with you. I'm not gonna hurt her."

With that, he stalked back inside his house.

Jen's eyes met mine, a fraction softer. "I'm sorry to get you involved in this, but he came home just before I called you and went completely psycho on me. He—"

King's voice bellowed from another room. "Jen, get your ass in here and stop fucking bitching."

She stiffened. "I don't know why the fuck I came back to him. I should have known things would never change."

I frowned. "You thought you and King would get back together?" She'd told me the other day she wished things could have been different between them, so I figured that meant they had no hope of reconciliation.

Her words were a mix of disappointment, hurt, and bitterness when she answered me. "I've always held out hope, Devil, but that man will never change. No woman will ever be able to compete with his first love and beat her for the top place in his heart."

I watched as she walked away, defeat clinging to her body so hard I wondered if she'd ever get over it.

I took hold of Hailee's hand. "You good, darlin'?"

She nodded, no hint of hesitation to be seen. "I'm good."

When we found King in his kitchen, he passed me a glass of rum. "Drink up, brother, you're gonna need it for what I'm about to tell you."

I took the drink and knocked back half of it. When King thought news was that bad I'd need alcohol to stomach it, I knew something was up.

King's eyes fell on Hailee. "Who are you?"

"Hailee." She sounded calm and unfazed by him, but her body was tense.

"And?" He clipped out. King wasn't known for his patience with the women club members dated. Not until they became official. Then, he had all the time in the world for them.

"And I'm hoping this won't take too long because Devil was about to take me home and fuck me before he received the call to come here," she said, her body losing some of its tenseness.

King stared at her in silence, his face blank. You could bet his mind wasn't blank, though. That brain of his would be processing thoughts at a rapid pace. Finally, he threw the remainder of his rum down his throat and said, "Jen, take Hailee into the lounge room. I want to talk to Devil alone."

Jen shot a look of anger King's way and started to say something, but King's face clouded over with a dark warning and he barked, "Now!"

Her face scrunched up and she spat out, "You can be a fucking asshole when you want to be."

King's eyes didn't leave her. "Yeah, well it takes a bitch to bring it out in me some days, and you've managed to hit the fucking motherload today." He tracked her movements as she exited the room, Hailee in tow. When we were alone, he jerked his chin towards the backyard and said, "We need to take this outside."

I followed him all the way to the middle of his yard. Darkness cloaked us and the heat of the night stuck to our skin. We were in the middle of a fucking heat wave in Sydney, and it wreaked havoc on my ability to think straight at times. However, my thoughts were clear as fuck. Something had spooked King and I sensed danger ahead.

"We found Shannon," he started. "He won't be a problem for anyone anymore. But he told me some of the shit that Jen told him while they were together, and it's likely to come back and bite us in the ass."

"Jesus, what did she tell him?"

"A lot of shit about how the club operates. Who supplied us back when she and I were together. Who our allies were, and our enemies, that kind of shit."

"A lot of that has changed, though, King. How will that hurt us? Especially if he's dead now."

His voice dropped. "She told him about Moses. And I'm guessing that if the feds are sniffing around about that, he's told them or someone else."

"Fuck." I raked my fingers through my hair, a sense of dread snaking through me. "Why the fuck would she tell him that? And what exactly did she know?"

"That's what we've been arguing about. She swears she was drunk when she told him and that she didn't tell him much at all. She doesn't know the full story of what happened, because I never told her, but I'm guessing she knew just enough to give the feds a fucking hard-on." He blew out a harsh breath. "I swear, women are more fucking hassle half the time than they're worth. I should have known that Jen was sneaking around the fucking club sniffing out gossip and information."

After spending time with Jen that week and seeing a different side to her, and then hearing her desperation tonight to reconcile with King, I paused for a moment while trying to take in all this new information. It would be easy to brand Jen as a malicious and vengeful bitch, and while she definitely fit that bill, I knew she was so much more complex than that. Not that giving her an inch of forgiveness would help the club, yet I couldn't quite bring myself to despise her completely.

"Okay, so we can't go back and change what's been said or done. And I know you, King, as much as you're angry with her now, you'll end up standing by her, for the baby's sake if nothing else. Which means that going another round with her is pointless. Why don't you let me talk to her and see what I can find out?"

He remained silent for a beat; the only sound coming from him was his angry breaths. His anger made me think he'd say no to my request, but he surprised me when he agreed. "That woman will be the absolute fucking death of me one day. I know that, yet I can never say no to her. I can scream at her until I'm fucking blue in the face and feel like my chest has been ripped open with rage and hate and love. And yet, I can't fucking say no." His words fell out of his mouth along with his anger. In the end, all he seemed to be left with was an overwhelming sense of powerlessness. It reminded me that the only time I'd ever seen him like that also involved Jen.

"I understand, brother."

And, I did. What he said about her dredged up my deeply buried feelings about my father. Feelings of hurt that were threaded with rage and hate and love also. However, just like King, I knew that if my father reached out to me now, even after fifteen years, and offered me hope that things could be different, I wouldn't be able to say no. Even though saying yes could destroy me.

"Talk to her, Devil. Find out what we need."

I headed back inside and found Jen and Hailee talking in the lounge room.

Jen glanced up at me. "Hailee has a wealth of knowledge about morning sickness. I'm hoping she might have the cure for me."

Jen and King were so fucking similar. I guessed that was why they clashed so much. They were the only people I knew who could go from one extreme of emotion to another in less than ten minutes. Gone was her anger and in its place was something close to calm and happy.

Hailee touched her arm gently. "That remedy hasn't worked for everyone I've told about it, but it has had some great results."

"What's the remedy?" King asked from behind me.

I stepped aside so he could join us. When he didn't enter the room, I glanced back at him to find his arms crossed over his chest and his hard stare back in place. While he seemed resigned to the truth of his relationship with Jen, it didn't appear that he was going to make it easy for either of them.

Jen's wary gaze lingered on him. "A glass of milk and a milk arrowroot biscuit before getting out of bed in the morning. We're not sure if it will help much in the afternoon, but I'm mostly sick in the morning now, so I'm hoping this will cure it."

King listened intently and then nodded before giving his attention to Hailee. "Hailee, I think it's time you and I had a chat. I figure that any woman Devil brings to my home must be one he intends spending some time with, which means she's also a woman I want to get to know."

Hailee's eyes revealed her surprise, but she didn't hesitate to stand and agree. The earlier apprehension I'd felt had eased and had been replaced with confidence that King would treat Hailee well.

Jen turned to me after they left and said, "He wants you to talk to me, doesn't he?" She sighed. "That seems to be his way of dealing with me these days."

I sat next to her. "He does, but it was my idea. Clearly, you two weren't getting anywhere."

Her caustic reply came straight back. "Clearly. But that's because he wasn't willing to listen to anything I had to say. Which, correct me if I'm wrong, seems to be King's go-to response when he doesn't get his own way. He's always been like that."

If I was going to get anywhere with her, I needed to ease her into this. "He does like things to go his way, Jen, but aren't we all like that? He's not perfect, that's for sure. But are you?"

She fired up at that. "No, but I never said I was!"

"I know. And I also know that he's hurt you deeply. I don't know the ins and out of it, and I don't want to know. But I do know that he cares about you, even when you feel like he doesn't."

Her body sagged and the spirit she'd brought to her fight with King, drained from her. "I know," she whispered, her voice close to breaking. A tear slid down her face. "I can't help myself from fighting with him. We just bring the worst out in each other sometimes. And then at other times, he's amazing and I remember why I love him so much." A guttural sob tore from her and she clapped her hands over her mouth as she looked at me in horror. "What have I done, Devil? He'll never forgive me for this."

I sat quietly and watched while she fell apart. There wasn't anything I could say in answer to her question. I didn't know what this would do to their relationship. I suspected he would forgive her, but maybe he'd simply stash it away as another knife to his heart and hope like hell he could still look at her without despising the shit she'd done to him and his club.

I reached for her hands and pulled them away from her face. "Jen, listen to me." When I had her attention, I continued, "What's done is done. You both have to figure out how to live with it, but the only way you're gonna do that is if you speak honestly and tell him, or me, exactly what you told Shannon. We need to know what we're dealing with here so we can put measures into place to protect the club and everyone involved."

She nodded, back and forth, over and over, like a crazed woman. Gulping back her hesitation, she said, "All I knew about Moses was that he was dumped on the club's doorstep one morning and that the club whore who birthed him killed herself later that day. The next thing I heard about it all was that the baby and the father went missing." She slid sideways on the chair, closer to me, and lowered her voice. "But I know that their disappearances weren't because the father took the baby and left. I heard King talking about it on the phone one night, saying that he had no clue what happened to the child, but that all the tracks were cleared up and no one would be able to prove a thing later on."

Fuck.

"And that's what you told Shannon?"

Fear radiated from her as she whispered, "Yes."

King was right to be worried, and I felt the distinct urge to drown in a bottle of rum. I stood. "I'll pass this info onto King." I struggled to look at her myself; I wasn't sure how King would manage it without wanting to throttle the life out of her.

Her fingers clawed at me, gripping my arm as I tried to leave. "Wait!" She stood. "What do you think King will do now that he knows all that?"

I raised a brow. "You're fucking kidding me, right?"

She remained silent.

Easing out of her grip, I said, "What do you think he's going to do, Jen? You betrayed his trust and you've put him and everything he values at risk. I think you know what he'll do." The thing was, though, that I figured he'd do what he already told me he'd do—he wouldn't be able to say no to her. Plus, he wouldn't leave a child to fend for itself with Jen as its mother.

She blinked rapidly a few times. "Yeah," she said with quiet unease.

I left her then and hoped I never had to see her again. Betrayal like she'd dealt to King wasn't something I could understand, and if she were in my life the way she was in his, I wasn't sure how I'd ever deal with it. Forgiveness would be a hard battle.

I found him and Hailee. She took one look at me and knew something was up. "I'll leave you two to it."

As he watched her go, King said, "I like her." He then turned to me. "But I'm not going to like what you're about to tell me, am I?"

I shook my head. "No."

After I relayed the information to him, he sat in silence for a long time before finally saying, "If she wasn't having a baby, I'd kick her out in a heartbeat." I felt every ounce of his dilemma. With one final glance at me, he said, "Why do we continue to love those who cut our hearts out and let them bleed all over the floor while telling us they really do love us?"

Chapter Sixteen

Hailee

I snuggled up to Devil and traced patterns on his belly. It was still early, somewhere around six, and he hadn't stirred. Usually he woke around that time, but this morning, he slept like the dead.

He'd been a little off after we'd left King's the night before. Whatever they'd been discussing had greatly affected him, King, and Jen. When we finished up there, none of them were talking. Devil and King seemed okay with each other, but neither man could look at Jen.

He'd even been subdued while we had sex. Rather than being wild and passionate, it had been slow and deep. Instead of looking at me like he wanted to consume every part of me like he usually did, his eyes had held something else all together. I'd felt like he was trying to read me. As if he'd been trying to figure something out. But we'd fallen asleep almost straight away, so I didn't get a chance to ask him about it.

"What secrets do you have buried deep?" I whispered as I kissed his chest.

I'd known him for almost two weeks and felt completely at ease with him. And yet, I hardly knew anything about him. Our relationship still felt right, though, and I hadn't experienced the usual new relationship nerves. I desperately wanted to know him on a deeper level, but I didn't want to push him to share anything he didn't want to. It wasn't the way I liked my relationships to go. If a guy wanted to take his time to open up to me, I could live with that so long as I felt he was invested. And Devil had made it abundantly clear he was invested.

He cut into my thoughts when he murmured, "Mornin'."

I almost jumped out of my skin when he spoke. Turning my face up to his, I found those eyes of his that saw everything, focused on me. The intense way he often watched me never failed to stir butterflies in my stomach. "Morning."

He placed his arm around me, sliding his hand down my back to rest just above my ass. "You sleep well?" God, how I loved his voice first thing in the morning. I mean, I loved it all the time, but particularly when it was husky from sleep.

Despite being skin-to-skin with him, I attempted to wriggle even closer. By the time I was done, I was practically lying on top of him. "I did. Did you? You were so tired."

"It's been a long week. I'm glad it's over, because now I've got you all to myself for two days."

I grimaced. "Well, I *do* have two massages I have to give and then I have that wedding to perform at tonight, remember? Which means I have to leave just after one to get there and set up. And that means I have to start getting ready at about eleven thirty."

"Fuck, it takes you an hour and a half to get ready? What do you have to do?"

I pulled a face and huffed at him. "I love how guys think women just magically appear all beautiful. Honestly, if you knew the number of hours we spend doing hair and make-up and getting dressed, you'd realise just how lucky you were to be born a male."

He grinned and pressed a quick kiss to my lips. "Keep talking dirty to me, gorgeous. You know my dick gets hard when you go all spitfire on me."

Ignoring him, I said, "So, that means we have about eight hours before I have to leave you. But I *am* free all day tomorrow."

His arm tightened around me as he said, "I'm counting on it."

That intrigued me. "Why? You got something planned?"

He ran his fingers lightly over my skin. "I thought I'd take you on a long ride up to The Entrance." A sexy smile spread across his face as he added, "Maybe get you in a bikini and spend the day in the sun."

I traced his lips with my fingertip and said, "A bikini, huh? What if I don't do bikinis?"

Lines creased his forehead as he frowned. "Why the fuck wouldn't you? Your body is made for a bikini, Hailee."

"Maybe I don't like men ogling me." I didn't. I hated it. And I hadn't worn a bikini since I was about fifteen.

"They wouldn't want to so much as look at you while you're with me." His mood darkened a little, and I knew that me wearing a bikini could be a very bad idea.

"Well, I don't own a bikini, so this whole conversation is a waste. Now, tell me, what did you and my brother discuss last night? We never did get around to talking about that." He'd told me we would talk about it when we got home, but after visiting King, that was all forgotten.

He stalled, and I thought maybe he would try to fob me off, but he didn't. "He gave me the usual grilling a brother gives his sister's new guy."

I would kill Aaron when I saw him next. "I'm sorry. He does this to every guy I see. He's a complete asshole to them and usually scares them off."

Devil rolled, taking me with him so that I ended up underneath him. Caging me in with his hands planted on the mattress either side of me, he said, "Nothing and no one is scaring me off, Hailee. Don't worry about your brother. He'll come around when he realises I'm not going to hurt you."

I hadn't realised that I was concerned about Aaron convincing Devil to walk away, but the relief that engulfed me when he said no one could scare him off told me otherwise.

Smiling up at him, I attempted to coax him into the shower. It was my preferred place for him to fuck me in the mornings. "I think we should move this to the shower."

He grinned, knowing exactly where my mind had gone. "You know I'm always down for that." He moved swiftly off the bed and I followed right behind, only to be caught by surprise when he lifted me over his shoulder to carry me into the bathroom. Chuckling at my surprise, he said, "And don't think I've forgotten about that bikini. I'm making it my mission to convince you that you should wear one."

As much as I had no intention of ever wearing one, I loved his determination. Or maybe it was just the fact that he really, really liked me and would go out of his way to show me. A girl needed that in her life, and it had been far too long since I'd had it.

***

"Put me down!" I squealed as Devil scooped me up into his arms and carried me from my lounge room to my bedroom. His eyes sparkled with devious intent as he ignored me and continued on.

We'd spent the morning together at his house, and he'd then brought me back to my place so I could get ready for work. Eleven thirty ticked closer on the clock, and I really only had five minutes until Dylan would arrive to pick me up. He'd agreed to be my chauffeur for the day.

"I'm not letting you go until you agree for me to pick you up after the wedding tonight," Devil said as he dumped me on my bed. We'd been going back and forth arguing over this, and he was being his usual demanding self.

I shifted so I could rest on my elbows while I stared up at him. "Why do you have to keep arguing with me over this? I've already organised for Dylan to bring me home. I could get him to drop me off at your place if that would make you happy."

"The only thing that's gonna make me happy is if I come pick you up myself. Give me the address and the time, and then you can go wait for Dylan."

"See that's the thing. I never really know what time I'll be done by. I mean, we're booked until eleven, but sometimes we're having so much fun that we just keep playing until they kick us out. So, it—"

He straddled me as he cut me off. "Darlin', the address," he said forcefully, and I knew it was time to just give in and give him what he wanted.

"Fine," I muttered, "but don't whinge when you're sitting there twiddling your thumbs waiting for me if we decide to stay."

"Jesus, woman, do you not think I'd happily sit for a day twiddling my thumbs while I waited for you?" His eyes searched mine before he dipped his face and caught my lips in a kiss.

I melted into his kiss in much the same way I basked in his words. And for the first time ever in my life of playing gigs with Cherry Vivid, I didn't want to play that night. I wanted to stay right where I was in Devil's arms.

When we came up for air, he stared down at me with lust-filled eyes. "I don't want you to go," he rasped. Sitting back, he shoved his fingers through his hair. "I'm so damn hard for you. Always, so fucking hard. Just thinking about you gets me there."

I reached for his shirt, gripping a handful. "I don't want to go either," I said, my voice just as affected as his.

After a few moments of silence, he finally moved off me and held his hand out to help me up. Slapping my ass, he said, "Come on, let's get you outside so I don't throw you down on that bed and fuck you so hard you won't be able to walk out of here."

I wanted exactly what he wanted, so it was safest to do what he'd said. As I exited the bedroom, the doorbell rang.

Thank you, God.

Dylan's timing was perfect.

However, when I opened the door, Dylan wasn't standing on the other side. Wayne was.

"Hailee," he greeted me with a smile.

Oh. God.

No.

No.

No.

I gripped the door while I sent at least ten urgent prayers up to God for him to give me an out. Right now. He could just let the floor cave in and allow me to slide into hell. Because that was where I should have been sent.

I was the worst person in the world.

I'd spoken to Wayne on the phone a few times while he was away.

When I'd started sleeping with Devil.

While I'd technically still been dating Wayne.

I hadn't wanted to string him along and lie to him, but telling someone you didn't want to see them again over the phone was a dick move. So I'd decided to wait until he arrived back home and then break the news to him.

I hadn't expected him to turn up on my doorstep unannounced.

While Devil was there.

Standing. Right. Behind. Me.

"Uh, Wayne. Hi." Fuck, could I sound any more pathetic? I was a tongue-tied mess. Not only that, I was sure sweat was about to drip from me. It was a hot day already, but my temperature had just doubled. At least.

Devil's hand slid around my waist as his body moulded to mine in one of the most possessive moves I'd ever experienced from a man. If I hadn't been so frazzled, I would have been turned on by it.

The smile in Wayne's eyes died as he tracked Devil's hand going around my waist and pulling me back against him. When he looked up, his gaze met mine briefly before he looked past me at Devil.

"Wayne," Devil said, his voice deep and gruff. *Dominant.*

Wayne's gaze flicked back to mine. "What's going on, Hailee?"

Anxiety burned in my chest. I hated confrontations. But even more than that, I hated hurting people. "I'm sorry, Wayne... I didn't want to tell you over the phone." I stumbled all over my words again, but I managed to get them out eventually.

"So, what? You're screwing him now?" Wayne shot his question at me like venom, and I recoiled.

Devil's other arm circled my chest and he held me tightly to him. "You can leave now, Wayne," he ordered. A shiver ran through me at the malevolence I heard in his tone. He was so calm, though. I wouldn't want to be in his firing line, because that kind of calm was more dangerous than fire.

Wayne ignored him. "I want a fucking answer, Hailee. Are you fucking him?" His eyes glittered with disgust, and I realised

I'd dodged a bullet with him. No way did I ever want to be involved with a man who treated me like that. Even if he did feel betrayed.

I'd hardly had time to process that thought when Devil switched our positions, putting himself in front of me. His calmness disappeared, replaced by a ferociousness I was yet to see in him.

"You ever speak to her that way again, and I'll make sure you never utter another word in your life. Now turn the fuck around and go the fuck back to where you came from."

My heart beat faster as I waited for Wayne to reply. Placing my hand on Devil's back, I found it hard as rock. He was wound so tight that I worried what his reaction might be if Wayne chose to argue with him rather than doing what he said.

"You know what I think?" Wayne spat out.

"What?" Devil's back tensed even more, like he was ready to lash out any minute.

I wished like crazy that I'd just been a dick and told Wayne over the phone. I didn't want Devil involved in this because it all seemed to be going to hell in a handbasket.

Wayne puffed up his chest. "I think she clearly doesn't know how to choose men. You're a pig, and there's no way you'd treat her as well as I would have. You two deserve each other."

He took a step back as if to leave, but Devil's hand shot out and grabbed him. Moving closer to him, Devil snarled, "And you know what *I* think, motherfucker? I think you know nothing about me and that you shouldn't be so quick to judge another person. I also think that if you don't leave right now, I won't be able to control myself much longer. My fist is fucking itching to smash itself into your face."

I'd never dated a guy as intense as Devil. His violent outburst frightened me, and I felt the need to stop him going any further. Especially since this was all my fault.

I cut through the tense air, inserting myself in front of Devil. I ignored the way he tried to pull me back, and placed my hand on his chest as if to say, "Back off." Eyeing Wayne, I said forcefully, "I'm sorry for the way this went down, but you need to accept my decision. And I think it would be best if you left now before this goes somewhere none of us want it to go."

He glared at me for what felt like longer than it probably was. I was so damn tense, worried that Devil would punch him, that it screwed with my concentration. I breathed the longest sigh of relief when he finally said, "Fine. I'm leaving. But don't come crawling back to me when you realise I was right."

A low growl sounded behind me as Devil pressed against my hand on his chest. But Wayne left us, and no harm came to pass. When I turned to face him, I found his angry eyes still following Wayne as he walked to his car.

I smacked his chest to gain his attention. "Devil."

He grunted, and I got the impression it was taking all his restraint not to go after Wayne.

Scrunching a handful of his shirt, I pulled on it. "Devil, stop. I don't want you doing something you might regret."

His eyes cut to mine, still angry. "Darlin', no way in hell would I fucking regret anything. That asshole needs to learn to shut his trap and not insult people."

"That's true, but honestly your response seemed a little over the top."

"It wasn't." Fury still flashed in his eyes, and I wondered where it came from. I struggled to believe Wayne caused it all. There had to be something else going on here that I didn't know about.

“You really believe that?” I knew bikers were renowned for using violence, but threatening Wayne in the manner he had seemed too much.

“We’re gonna have to agree to disagree on this one, Hailee.” He forced the words out on a harsh breath, unable to let his outrage go.

“Yeah, well I’m just telling you that I’m not a fan of unnecessary violence. You know my history with that. I don’t know anything about your club and what goes on there, but if we’re gonna keep dating, I’d rather you didn’t bring your temper home.” I pushed past him and went back inside. The confrontation between him and Wayne had really shaken me up, and I needed a moment to get myself together.

He didn’t follow me inside, so I guessed he needed the same thing. It was the first disagreement we’d had, and while we hadn’t really fought about it, I felt like this could turn into a problem for us. Devil was a biker after all and I hadn’t really stopped to think about that too much since I’d met him.

Chapter Seventeen

Devil

"So you let your temper get the best of you?" Sonya asked as she chopped vegetables for dinner.

After Hailee had left for work, I'd gone for a long ride to clear my head and then found myself at Sonya's place. The kids had been a good distraction for the afternoon, and she'd asked me to stay for dinner.

"Yeah." I'd just finished telling her about the way I'd reacted to Wayne when he showed up at Hailee's home.

She glanced up at me. "Why? We worked so hard on getting it under control, and I thought you were doing better. Why all of a sudden did you snap?"

Just thinking about Wayne stirred my anger again. I took a couple of deep breaths while I tried to work through it. "I can't explain it. Well, not the initial trigger. That seemed to come from an urge to protect Hailee. But after that, when he started badmouthing both of us, it sparked all those old feelings of being worthless that Dad used to make me feel. It put me right back there with him." Sonya was the only person I ever spoke so honestly with about all this shit. Having been my brother's high school sweetheart, we'd grown up together and she'd lived through my hell with me.

Anger to me was like alcohol to an alcoholic. Or at least it had been for more than a decade. I'd used it to numb the hurt and the shame of not feeling wanted by my parents.

I held Sonya's gaze while I said, "What kind of parent wants a child enough to create them, and then abandons that child when they decide it isn't good enough for them? How can a father do that to his son?" He'd kicked me out of home and ran me out of town when he didn't approve of my choices in life. And I still lived with that hurt.

She stopped chopping the carrots and put her knife down. Moving to me, she enveloped me in a hug and said, "Ivan Ford is a fool, Dom. We've already discussed this. Why are you allowing yourself to be dragged back down by him?"

It always felt safe with Sonya. *She* was my safe place. Even though Campbell took issue with my choices in life and made it hard for me to be close to his family, she'd never once let me down. We'd spent the last few years working on my temper and angry outbursts, and she'd guided me every step of the way. Her mother was a psychologist in Tamworth, and Sonya had relied on her advice to help me. However, regardless of all that, my internal walls were up, and I couldn't access my own damn feelings. I didn't know why this was all surfacing.

I moved out of her embrace. "I have no fucking clue. I haven't heard from him or even really been thinking of him lately, so I don't know why all of a sudden he's in my fucking head."

She turned quiet for a moment, thinking. "Maybe it's finally time for you to go back," she said softly.

"You're not serious?" She couldn't be. "You've seen the way Campbell still treats me. He gets that from Dad. Campbell fucking hangs off every word Dad says, so there's no way in hell Dad has changed his mind where I'm concerned if Campbell still thinks that way. And besides, I have no interest in going back there.

"I'm not suggesting you go back because anything has changed with your father. I'm suggesting it because maybe *you* need the closure. I think you've been holding on all these years hoping he'd come to his senses. You need to see for yourself what his thoughts on the matter are now. And then hopefully you can either close that door or decide you're okay with still leaving it open."

"That fucking door *is* closed." It fucking slammed shut years ago when he ran me out of the town I grew up in.

Kylie ran into the kitchen then, flying straight into me. Her little arms wrapped around my legs as she squealed, "Uncle Dom, you're still here!" Sonya had put Kylie and her brother to bed earlier, and she'd been upset at the thought of me not being there when she woke up.

I pulled her up into my arms and gave her a huge smile. "Of course I am, baby girl. I told you I would be."

She almost choked me in a hug as she squished her arms around my neck. "I wanna go on the swing!"

I met Sonya's gaze. "You need me to help with dinner?"

She shook her head. "No, you guys go play. It'll give me some peace and quiet."

"Okay," I said to Kylie, "let's go find your brother. We'll play for a bit and then it's bath time before dinner."

Her glee was infectious. Fuck, I loved playing with kids. They made me forget all the ugly shit in the world. "Yay, yay, yay!"

That excitement and the love she never failed to give me was exactly the medicine I needed after spending the afternoon beating myself up.

I pressed a kiss to her forehead as I carried her out of the kitchen. "I love you, kid."

She buried her face in my neck. "I love you, too, Uncle Dom."

Exactly what I needed.

***

My Sunday plans to get Hailee into a bikini had to be changed when she woke with a sore throat and fever. She could hardly move, so I figured there was no getting out of bed for her.

I placed my hand on her forehead and frowned. "No bikini for me today."

"I told you, there is no bikini for you ever," she croaked.

I fought a smile and bent to give her a quick kiss. "Oh, there will be a bikini. I'll make sure of it."

She groaned and pushed me away. "Don't come too close. You'll get sick, too."

I scowled. Moving my face back near hers, I ignored what she said. "What do you need, darlin'? Asprin? Advil?" I grinned as I added, "Cock?"

She smiled at that. "As much as I want your dick, and as much as I think it has magical powers, I really doubt it will cure the headache I have or ease my sore throat. But I'll take a raincheck, okay?"

Sliding my hand down her body, I reached for her pussy. "I could just—"

She slapped my hand away. "God, you're gonna drive me crazy today, aren't you?"

Laughing, I admitted, "Maybe."

"Okay, well let's start with some Advil. If that helps, we might move onto cock." Even through her sickness, she couldn't hide her amusement, giving me an eye-roll that was mixed with a shake of her head.

I pushed up off the bed. "I'm on it."

When I came back to her with a glass of water and pills, I found her curled almost into a ball while she had a coughing fit. Sitting next to her, I waited for her coughs to subside before passing her the glass and tablets. "What else can I do besides the pills, darlin'?"

She sat up enough so she could swallow the tablets. "Hold me while we watch a movie together?"

I switched the television in the bedroom on, positioned her next to me on the bed, and held her close while we watched *Marley and Me*. It was the absolute worst movie choice because it made her cry and hurt her throat.

But it was the perfect movie choice because she snuggled against me and told me how much she loved that I'd listened to her when she told me that was her favourite movie.

***

Hailee was sick in bed for three days. I spent that time taking care of club business during the day and looking after her at night. I moved her back to her home on Monday afternoon after I finished up with club work. She was hardly conscious that night, so I had dinner with Jean, listening to stories of the crazy shit Hailee got up to when she was younger, before spending the night taking care of Hailee.

Tuesday night, I cooked dinner after arriving and finding Jean not feeling well. I sent her to the couch to rest after making sure she'd had painkillers. Hailee was awake in her bed but didn't have the energy to eat dinner at the table, so I took it into her.

She hit me with a smile as I passed her a bowl of soup. "Thank you," she croaked. She'd told me her throat wasn't sore anymore. It had left her with a raspy throaty voice that did amazing shit to my dick.

I sat next to her. "You like chicken soup?"

She glanced at the soup before looking back at me. "Did you make this?"

"Yeah."

Her eyes widened in surprise. "Wow."

"I told you my sister taught me to cook. Chicken soup was one of those things."

She stared at me with a stunned expression.

When she didn't speak, I said, "I know you're sitting there thinking how fucking amazing I am. I mean, not only am I good at using my dick, I'm good in the kitchen, too."

Shaking her head at me, she muttered, "You really are too much sometimes. Let me taste it and see if you're as talented in the kitchen as you are in bed."

I smirked but didn't say another word while I waited for her thoughts on my cooking.

Her eyes lit up as she had her first taste. She quickly ate more and was halfway through the bowl when she finally said, "Oh my God, you can fucking cook. This is the best chicken soup ever. I need to meet your sister so I can thank her for teaching you some mad skills."

I lifted a brow. "You ever gonna doubt me again, darlin'?"

"Don't go getting ahead of yourself, bossman. A girl's gotta make sure of these things sometimes. In fact"—she handed me the empty bowl—"I think I need to test it some more. You know, just to be sure."

I took the bowl and stood, grinning. "If you're fucking well enough to run me around after you, I think you're well enough to give my dick some action tonight."

"Ha," she said with a laugh that turned into a cough. "I could probably lie there while you do your thing, but this mouth isn't up to sucking or anything like that, so don't go getting excited."

"I'll take a hand job," I threw over my shoulder as I exited the room.

The tension I'd been carrying in my shoulders and neck due to the stress with the club started to ease thanks to Hailee. The last week had been spent trying to figure out Wesley Marx's game. We'd also tried to work out what the feds had on us over Moses. Bronze was helping with that, but even he struggled to find out what we needed to know. King was furious with Jen and had started sleeping at the clubhouse, leaving me to deal with her. On top of that, Bronze had pulled me aside yesterday to tell me again to leave his sister alone. Nothing had been resolved with any of these things, and the stress was beginning to show in the club. I was fucking grateful to have Hailee to come home to at night. She couldn't fix my problems for me, but just being with her helped me forget them for a while.

***

Shit with the club came to a head on Thursday afternoon when Bronze turned up at the clubhouse, furious.

"Two things," he bellowed after King had ushered him, Nitro, and me into his office. He held up one finger. "Firstly, I've been able to confirm the feds are indeed investigating your club over the Moses thing and they're also looking into your drug activity." He turned to me and held up a second finger. "And secondly, you put fucking railings on Hailee's house even after I told you to stop fucking seeing her. I wasn't mucking around, Devil. Either stop seeing her or I'll fucking walk away from this club and cut all ties."

My temper exploded at the same time Nitro's did. We both responded with an angry outburst, but King cut through the noise we both made with—"Enough!" When all three of us stopped and stared at him in furious silence, he rubbed his temple and said, "For fuck's sake, I've got the headache from hell. I've had no fucking sleep for days, we're dealing with fucking crisis after crisis, and you wanna bring this shit to me? What the fuck, Bronze?"

Bronze's eyes blazed with fury. "My sister mightn't be important to you, but she's fucking important to me, and I refuse to allow Devil to drag her into your world."

King frowned. "Hailee's your sister?"

"Yes!" Bronze squared his shoulders. "I will walk, King, and I won't fucking look back."

King's nostrils flared as his body tensed. "Like fuck you'll walk."

"I give no shits about the cash you give me. I'd give all that up without a second fucking thought."

King took a step closer to him. The dangerous glint in his eye matched the deadly energy vibrating from him. "And I give no fucks about the cash either. What I *do* care about, though, is what I did for you seven years ago. Has that shit vanished from your memory? Do you need me to remind you about that? About what it would mean for your life and your career?"

Bronze's lips flattened as he stared at King with resentment. "Maybe it's time for me to pay for my sins."

"You don't want to pay for those sins, Bronze. You'd fucking die at the hands of all the motherfuckers you've helped lock up if you went to jail now."

"Maybe I'd rather die than have Hailee's safety compromised."

They stared at each other in silence for a long few moments before I finally stepped in. "Her safety isn't compromised."

Bronze's head whipped around so he faced me. Snarling, he said, "It mightn't be yet, but I've seen the shit your club gets involved with, and I don't want her anywhere near that."

I opened my mouth to reply, but King's venomous voice sliced through the air. "You talk a good fucking game, Bronze, but I think we both know that you are so far entrenched in the activities of this club that you could spend an eternity trying to climb your way out and you'd not come close to escaping. I've heard enough of this bullshit. Get me more info on what the feds know." With that, he stalked out of the office, leaving Bronze staring after him.

"Hailee's happy with me, Bronze. Think about that before you try to take it all away from her," I snapped before exiting the office also. If I didn't leave then, I wasn't sure I'd be able to stop myself from trying to knock him the fuck out.

I found King in the bar with a drink in front of him. Eyeing me as I approached, he said, "I'd suggest you stay clear of me today. I'm in a foul fucking mood, and I'm more than fucking ready to get into it with someone."

I ignored him and indicated for Kree to bring me a drink. "You need to go home and get some sleep, King. And while you're there, you need to talk to Jen. She's losing her shit, and I'm concerned for the baby."

His eyes darkened. Throwing some of his drink back, he said, "If I go home before I get my mind straight, you'll be fucking worrying about more than that baby. No fucking way am I setting foot in that house this week."

Fuck.

"I'm telling you, she's not coping." This was the last fucking conversation I wanted to be having, but I'd found Jen on the bathroom floor that morning holding a knife. The way she'd been staring at that knife led me to believe she intended to harm herself. And as much as I hated what she'd done to King, and agreed with his anger towards her, I knew he'd never forgive himself if that baby died because of something he could have helped stop. I'd managed to talk her down this time and was increasing my visits to her, but what she really needed was him.

He slammed his hand down on the top of the bar and roared, "And I'm fucking telling you that she should have fucking thought of that before she betrayed me." He drained his glass and slammed it down, too. "Fuck!" With his eyes boring into mine, he said, "I want to wrap my hands around her fucking throat and strangle her last breath out of her, Devil. You still think I should go see her?"

I shoved my fingers through my hair, unsure of what to suggest. Nitro's voice sounded from behind us. "Devil and I will go with you."

King swivelled to face him. "What, to save Jen's life?" He spat. "You really think the two of you could stop me from doing something I've spent the last six nights dreaming of doing? No fucking way, Nitro."

Nitro stepped closer. "I know you, King, and I know how much you love that woman. You might scream at her, and spew your hate at her, but you'll never hurt her physically."

King forced out an angry breath. Without looking at her, he barked, "Kree! I need another fucking rum."

She dropped what she was doing and quickly made him a drink. He emptied the glass in one go before saying, "Devil, this thing with Hailee, is it serious?"

I nodded. "Yeah, it is."

"Fuck," he muttered. "Was really fucking hoping you'd say no."

Nitro's phone rang, distracting him, and he moved away from us to take the call.

King watched him for a moment. "I'll never make the same mistake I made with Nitro by not listening to what you have to say, but I'm asking if you could tone it down with Hailee while we wade through this shit with the feds. I've got enough dirt on Bronze to use in an effort to convince him not to walk away from the club, but I'm not getting the vibe from him that he gives a fuck about the consequences of that."

I wasn't either. The last thing I wanted to do was what he'd asked. However, my loyalty to him and the club caused me to rethink that. "You think Bronze can keep us out of the shit with the feds?" He'd looked after us for years, burying evidence and keeping us safe from prosecution, but he didn't work for the federal police so I wasn't sure how far his reach extended.

King nodded, though. "Bronze has people everywhere, Devil. He's good for this. He walks, we're fucked."

Nitro came back to us while I thought about what King had said. "That was Hyde." He met King's gaze. "I asked him to keep an eye on Ghost's sister. They just turned up at her house and she's gone."

"Gone, as in skipped town?" King asked.

"Yeah, as in her house is empty and we don't know where she is." His voice hardened. "As in it looks like Ghost is trying to keep her safe."

There was only one reason why Ghost would want to keep her safe.

"Jesus fucking Christ!" King's temper flared again. "Find her! And while you're at it, let's, for the love of fuck, find out what the hell Wesley Marx's game is!"

Chapter Eighteen

Hailee

I sat in my car outside my mother's home late Friday afternoon dreading the thought of going inside. She'd called last night demanding I join her for dinner. The fact I was still recovering from being sick wasn't enough to get out of it. I could have said no, but that would only have lead to her bitching about my refusal for months. It was far easier to suck it up and go.

My phone sounded with a text.

Leona: You there yet, babe?

Me: Ugh. Yes. Send luck.

Leona: Luck!

Me: Tell me something good. I need that to get me through the night.

Leona: Jerry fucked me the minute I walked in from work. I'm fairly sure I'm pregnant now.

Me: Why?

Leona: He never has sex without planning it. This is a whole new thing for us.

Me: So you think his sperm are partying with your eggs because of his spontaneity?

Leona: LOL Yes!

Me: Okay that was good. Every time my mum pisses me off tonight, I'll think of your baby.

Leona: Love you, Hails.

Me: Love you. Now go have sex again just to be sure.

A tap on the car window caused me to jump as I shoved my phone back in my bag. Looking up, I found Aaron bent over looking at me.

Opening the door, I muttered, "Fuck, Aaron, way to give a girl a heart attack."

He narrowed his eyes at me. "You paid your rego?"

I rolled my eyes as I got out of the car. He was asking from a cop perspective. All his rules and regulations pissed me off. Sometimes, I'd just like him to be laid-back about stuff. "Yes, I paid it yesterday if you must know."

He stepped back to let me out. "Christ, did you have a bad day?"

I slammed the door and then glared at him. "Yeah. It turns out my brother doesn't like my boyfriend, so my mum refused to invite him to dinner, which means I have to sit through this fucking night by myself."

"I'm here, Hailee. You're not on your own."

I stared at him. "God, you have no idea."

He blew out a frustrated breath. This was our same old argument. Without fail, we always had it when we visited Mum. "Tell me, what do I have no idea about this time?"

I straightened my shoulders, ready to lay it all out, when Mum called out from her veranda, "Aaron, come inside, it's hot out here."

My brows shot up and I jabbed a finger in her direction. "*That* for one. No worries about Hailee being fucking hot!"

I stalked away from him, up to where Mum stood waiting. Her mouth spread out into a thin smile for me as I approached, before her gaze darted to Aaron and her smile grew.

"Hi, Mum," I greeted her as Aaron's boots sounded on the step behind me.

"Hailee," she murmured, running her eyes down my body as a scowl appeared on her face. I guessed she didn't like the short shorts I'd worn that night. Or maybe it was the skimpy white T-shirt I'd paired them with. The one that clung to my boobs in the way I knew she hated.

She quickly transferred her attention to my brother. Her gushing over him sickened me, so I left them and entered the house.

My gaze fell on the family portrait that had always hung in the entryway. The portrait of the three of us with Dad and Gran. *The fucking portrait that had disappeared and been replaced with a framed family photo that didn't include Gran.*

Turning back to Mum, I demanded, "Where's the family portrait?"

She looked at me with distaste. "I beg your pardon? Since when do you come into my home and speak to me in that manner?"

I ignored her question. "I can't believe the way you've acted since Dad died. You were just itching to cut Gran out, weren't you?"

"Hailee," Aaron said in a deep voice full of warning.

My phone buzzed with a text, and because I was waiting to hear from Devil, I quickly flicked it over in my hand so I could read the message.

Leona: Sperm. Babies. Happy times. You've got this, girl.

Fucking fuckity fuck.

What the fuck was I doing? I never won an argument with my mother. Fucking never. So why bother trying now?

Just take a deep breath, Hailee, and get through this night. You won't have to see her again for another three months if you're lucky.

With another glare at Aaron, I turned and made the long trek down the hallway to the dining room where I knew Mum would be serving dinner.

This house was way too big for her. She kept it because it had been in her family for years. I figured she had plans to leave it to Aaron when she passed away. Good luck to him, because all I could think was the amount of cleaning it needed. That wasn't something I ever wanted in my life.

Mum served dinner ten minutes later. At least I could always count on her not to fuck around and keep us waiting. She was a stickler for being on time, and when she said dinner was at six, you arrived at six and you were eating by quarter past. This was good for me because it meant I had half a shot at being out of there by seven thirty.

She'd cooked a roast lamb and vegetables, and my guess was she had apple pie and cream for dessert. *So damn predictable.* My life had run on predictability while I grew up. It was one reason why I left the country and travelled as soon as I could.

"Hailee." Aaron's voice broke into my thoughts. I glanced up to find him staring at me as if he was waiting for an answer to a question.

"Huh?"

My mother tsked. "I asked you how your work was going?"

She didn't really want to know. Usually I'd give her the standard reply that all was well so she could move straight onto Aaron who she actually *was* interested in, but I'd had some exciting news that day, and I decided to share it with them. "I received a phone call today from a woman who wants to invest in my charity work."

Mum stared at me blankly while Aaron smiled and said, "That's fantastic. Who is she?"

"She's the CEO of a superannuation company here in Australia. Her aunt's friend has been receiving massages from me, and she heard about it that way. She wants to meet with me next week to talk about investing the kind of money that would mean I could run it full time." *And leave Rachel and her awfulness behind.*

"Really?" Mum asked in the condescending manner she often used on me.

"Really, what?" I actually had no clue what she meant, other than perhaps she was questioning the truth in what I'd said.

Mum put down her cutlery and trained her disbelieving gaze on me. "I keep waiting for the day you come home and tell me some good news. And it never happens."

Her words were like a punch to my gut. In one way, they hurt more than the physical punches I'd received at the hands of Mickey years ago. "What kind of news would you like to hear, Mum?" I was proud of myself for maintaining my cool even when my heart screamed at me to tell her how much she'd hurt me.

"Well, for one, I wish you would give up this silly idea to run a massage charity. I mean, *really*. Why can't you just go back to university and finish the business degree you started? And two, you're thirty, Hailee. Don't you think it's time you started to look for a good catholic man to settle down with?"

My eyes almost bugged out of my head.

Aaron cut in, though, before I could reply to her bullshit. "Jesus, Mum, when are you going to just let her be? She's happy. Isn't that all that matters?" His words came out harshly, and I was taken aback. I'd never once heard him talk to our mother that way. I was also secretly fucking impressed with him. He'd stood up for me often, but mostly he just preferred to keep the peace. This, for him, was going above and beyond.

Mum stared at him like she'd just been slapped. "I will not tolerate that kind of language in my house, Aaron."

I shoved my chair back. I'd heard enough. "Oh for fuck's sake, Mum, you need to move into the twenty-first century. I'm not searching for a good catholic man just so I can improve my social standing by turning my spinster status around. I know you're embarrassed that I'm thirty and not married, but I'm not. I'm actually quite happy being single. Although, I guess you know now from Aaron that I'm dating a biker. The good news, though, is that he's catholic."

She blanched.

"No, I hadn't told her that," Aaron murmured.

I shrugged. "Oh well, she had to find out sooner or later."

Mum's hand moved to her throat while she processed everything I'd said. "Tricia said you'd changed, but I didn't want to believe it."

"Oh God, not this again. When did she say that?" My ex-best friend refused to cut ties with my family, and it pissed me off.

"She came for morning tea this morning, and we discussed your desire—"

I held up my hand to stop her. "I'm not interested in what you two discussed. If you can't see that she treated your daughter badly, then that makes me really sad. Most mothers would want the kind of friend who cheered their daughter on in everything she did in life. They wouldn't want one like Tricia, who was jealous of my new success and new friends." I picked up my bag. "Thank you for dinner, but I'm not hungry anymore."

I didn't wait for her response.

I fled my family home as fast as I could with no intention of going back anytime soon.

***

By the time I arrived on Devil's doorstep half an hour later, tears streamed down my cheeks, and I was fairly certain it looked like an artist had painted messy black lines down those cheeks.

I'd cried all the way from Mum's house to his. Long shuddering sobs. The worst thing was I had no tissues on me or in the car, so the only thing I'd been able to use was the white T-shirt I wore.

Devil's concerned gaze travelled down my face to my shirt and back up to my eyes. "Fuck, darlin', what happened?" He reached out and pulled me inside to his lounge room where he positioned me on his lap. His strong arms around me were exactly what I needed, but instead of soothing me, it only made me cry harder.

I buried my face in his neck and clung to him. He didn't push me to speak but simply comforted me and waited until I was ready.

I cried for a long time. Decades' worth of tears fell, and when I finally lifted my head to find his eyes, I felt like a weight had lifted. The heaviness that was my mother would never be lifted completely, but these tears had been a long time coming, and it felt good to shed them.

"Thank you," I whispered, barely able to see him through my wet lashes.

"You want some tissues?"

I nodded. "Yeah."

He shifted me onto the couch so he could stand and leave to go in search of the tissues. When he returned, he held the box out to me before sitting and pulling me back onto his lap.

"I take it dinner with your mother didn't go well."

I cleaned my face enough so I could see, and tried to remove some mascara from my cheeks. “Let’s just say that I don’t think she’s going to invite me back anytime soon. And let’s also say that I don’t give a flying fuck.”

“What happened?”

I proceeded to tell him everything that had gone down that night. Even the fact that I thought he’d never be welcome in my mother’s home because he was a biker. More tears gushed while I told him, and I wondered if they would ever stop. My relationship with Mum had always been hard, but after that dinner, I was finally facing just how bad it was.

“I really don’t want to see her again,” I whispered to Devil after I finished telling him everything. “Not ever.”

His arm tightened around me. “You might see things differently tomorrow.”

I shook my head. “I don’t think so. I think I’m done.”

He nodded, accepting what I said without trying to make me change my mind. I loved that he simply listened without offering advice.

We sat in silence for a long time. He held me while I thought about everything that had happened again.

When I sighed and rested my head against his chest, he said, “Fuck anyone who doesn’t think you should pursue your dreams, Hailee. I’m fucking happy for you, darlin’.”

I slid my hand up his shirt to his throat and then to his face. Placing my palm flat to his cheek, I lifted my head and smiled at him. “Thank you. You have no idea what that means to me.”

He brushed a kiss across my lips and murmured, “Fuck, you’re beautiful. Even when your face is puffy as shit and your makeup is all over the place.”

His compliment caused butterflies in my tummy. I shifted to straddle him with my knees pressed into the couch either side of his legs. Taking hold of his face, I said, "How is it that I can be crying my heart out one minute and the next you're making me want to kiss you?"

A lazy smile spread across his face. "I'm just talented like that." His hands cupped my ass. "You should definitely kiss me."

"Should I?" I teased, wanting more than anything to have him help me forget my mother.

Gripping my ass, he slid me closer to him so that my pussy pressed against his erection. His eyes glazed over with desire as he growled, "Yes."

I didn't waste any more time. Lowering my mouth to his, I kissed him for so long I thought our mouths might never come apart again. When he finally dragged his mouth from mine, I was breathless and desperate to be skin-to-skin with him.

"I need you," I begged, my voice husky and my heart fluttery.

He didn't need to be told twice.

Holding me tightly, he stood, taking me with him. The look of determination in his eyes as he carried me down his hallway told me I was about to have some amazing sex. And that he was going to do exactly what I needed—wipe all thoughts of my mother from my mind.

Chapter Nineteen

Hailee

Devil was blowing my damn mind.

After I'd asked him to fuck me, he'd scooped me into his arms and carried me into the bathroom. He'd then taken his sweet time undressing me with slow, gentle movements.

Once he had me naked, he reached into the shower cubicle and turned the water on. Stepping inside, he pulled me in with him, his hands sliding over my hips and around to my ass so he could pull me against him.

His eyes dipped to my mouth, and he bent to kiss me.

My knees buckled at the way his lips gently deepened the kiss. There was none of his usual dominance. The rough and dirty way he liked to take me with his mouth was nowhere to be seen. Instead, he consumed me with devotion. Worshipping my body and my heart. *Treasuring me.*

Breathless when he ended the kiss, I whispered, "There are so many parts to you, aren't there?" He'd shown me his bossy side, his flirty fun side, and his intense side. This tenderness peeled back a whole other layer.

His fingers dug into my ass. Not answering what I said, he asked, "You want it gentle or rough? My preference is to slam you up against that wall and fuck you six ways from Sunday, but if you want me to keep going slow, I can do that, too."

Oh, God, I wanted it all. Gentle. Rough. Long. Hard. I ran my fingers through his hair and scrunched a handful of it, pulling hard. "I want both."

He hissed. Keeping one hand on my ass, he reached for my hair with the other and yanked my head back, exposing my neck to him. His teeth sunk into my skin near my throat and he bit and sucked me. When he finished, he rasped, "Fuck, baby, I can't get enough of you."

He then turned us so that I stood under the water. Picking up the shower sponge, he filled it with shower gel and started washing me. Gentle strokes cleaned every inch of me, and a couple of minutes later, he kneeled in front of me as he ran the sponge over my thighs.

His breaths quickened as the air surrounding us thickened with our desire. Steam filled the room, and water ran down my body while I watched him take care of me.

He nudged my legs apart before draping one of them over his shoulder. When his tongue flicked against my clit a second later, I reached one hand out to lean against the shower wall in an effort to steady myself while I gripped his hair with my other hand.

I was still recovering from him calling me baby when he began delivering the kind of pleasure that rocked my world. The way baby rolled off his tongue was bewitching. Without realising it, he'd cast a spell over me. I would do whatever he wanted that night. And when he backed it up with his special kind of ecstasy, I was all but owned.

One hand on my ass.

His tongue buried deep inside.

Lips sucking my clit.

Husky sounds filling my ears.

It was sensory overload of the best kind, and I had to work hard to catch my breath because it was almost too much.

Devil stayed on his knees blessing my pussy for so long I wasn't sure I'd be able to hold myself up much longer. Mostly because my legs had turned to jelly, but also because he had blown my damn mind to the point I couldn't think straight enough to continue standing.

When I finally came, after he edged me closer, over and over, I cried out, "Oh, God, fuck!" My body swayed as my eyes squeezed closed and my head rolled back.

I'm going to collapse.

I can't take any more.

It's too much.

As my legs buckled, Devil's arm snaked around my waist, and he caught me. Holding me up, he walked me backwards until I hit the wall behind me.

I opened my eyes right as his lips crashed down onto mine.

He gave me no time to recover from the first orgasm he'd given. Instead, he started working on the second one.

Mouth on mine, hands everywhere, his erection grinding into me, Devil switched from slow and gentle, to rough and demanding.

Our movements soon turned frantic.

Him lifting me.

Me clinging to him.

Nails digging into his skin.

His teeth biting and marking me.

My mouth sucking on his neck.

His hands and mouth all over my breasts.

Both panting.

"Fuck, Devil, I need you in me." I could hardly get the words out in between breaths. When he didn't lift his mouth off my breast, I demanded, "Now! I need your cock inside me now."

His wild eyes finally met mine. "We need a condom."

When he made moves to put me down, I gripped him hard. "I'm clean."

His eyes searched mine, knowing what I was saying. Exhaling a breath, he nodded.

And then he was inside me.

Deep inside me.

Our bodies moved in perfect unison while we both chased our release. I held on tight for the ride and thanked God that he had decided to fuck me the way he always did. I loved slow and gentle, but I fucking lived for the thrill of rough sex.

Devil worked hard to bring me to orgasm before he let himself come. He held on so long that by the time he finally allowed his own release, he roared it out. His legs and back tensed as he thrust inside me one last time and came.

I was drowning in bliss by then. When he'd recovered enough to speak, he tilted my face to his and said, "Jesus fucking Christ, woman, you know how to fuck."

I smiled lazily, unable to give him much more than that. "And you have such a way with words."

He grinned. "How are those legs of yours? You good to walk or do you need me to carry you?"

I tightened my arms around him. "You should carry me. I think you fucked my ability to stand out of me. But I need to clean up first."

He brushed a kiss across my lips as he turned the shower off. "Okay, darlin'."

He let me down and stepped out of the shower, leaving me to clean myself up. When I exited the bathroom, he lifted me back into his arms and carried me to his bed. Sleep was claiming me after a long day and night. I drifted off with my body wrapped around Devil's and him whispering the dirty things he wanted to do to me. The last thing I remembered hearing was him saying, "I'm going to make you the happiest fucking woman on earth."

Chapter Twenty

Devil

I watched Hailee sleep from the doorway of my bedroom early the next morning. She'd woken me just after five when she rolled into me, flinging her arm over my chest and gripping her hand around my bicep. She hadn't been awake, but it was as if she was trying desperately to hold onto me. I let her hold me for as long as she wanted, and when she shifted again about an hour later, I'd managed to extricate myself so I could take a piss.

Her fucking mother had a lot to answer for. When Hailee had turned up crying the night before, I'd wanted to simultaneously make it all better for her while going over to her mother's and giving her a piece of my mind. I had no time for fucking parents who couldn't love their children unconditionally.

Hailee stirred, mumbling something I couldn't understand. Moving to the bed, I sat on the edge and ran my hand over her hair. Her beauty blew me away every fucking day. Not only her outer beauty, but also the inner glow she had. I wasn't sure I'd ever met anyone as kind as she was. The way she cared for people and animals amazed the fuck out of me.

"Morning," she mumbled as her eyes fluttered open.

"Morning, darlin'."

She shifted onto her side, curling her legs around me and placing her hand on my leg. "What time is it?"

Fuck, her voice was all fucking raspy from sleep, and it was waking my dick right the fuck up.

"It's early, just after six. I wasn't sure if you had work on today and whether you wanted to squeeze some meditation in before you went." Fuck knew, she could probably do with some of that after the shit her mother put her through.

She blinked a couple more times before she stared wide-eyed at me. Sitting up, she climbed into my lap and wrapped her arms and legs around me. "You better be careful there, bossman, or you might just make it so that you're stuck with me for life."

"I have no fucking idea what I did to make you climb me like you wanna ride me, but whatever it was, you need to tell me so I can do that shit again."

She shook her head with a devious grin. "Nope, I can't help you out too much. If I give all the secrets away, you'll stop working for it."

"Right," I said as I stood with her wrapped around me. "You need to either fuck me or climb down and let me go take care of business myself. And for the record, I don't plan on stopping working for it anytime soon, darlin'." I really fucking hoped she had time for sex, because my dick was so damn hard for her.

She didn't let go, which I took as a good sign. "I have to start work at eight thirty. I can skip my meditation if you want."

"I think we both know my answer to that." Fuck, I was a bastard. I knew how important her meditation was to her, but damn if my cock didn't need her more.

She moved for me to let her down. Lifting the T-shirt of mine she wore over her head, she threw it on the bed and said, "Just so you know, I'd choose your dick over meditation any day."

Fuck, she was the right fucking woman for me.

***

"Heard from Dragon this morning," King said to Hyde and me later that day when we were out following up a lead on Marx. "Swears he knows nothing about Marx and told me he'd put the feelers out, too."

Hyde scowled. "I don't trust that motherfucker."

King shook his head. "Agreed."

I didn't trust the president of Silver Hell either.

We were on our way to a bar where Eric Bones would be meeting us to pass on some information regarding Marx. King stopped and said, "I've got a feeling we're not going to be dealing with Gambarro anytime soon."

Hyde nodded as if he'd had the same thought. "Yeah, I don't think so either. These fucking feds are going to be all over us until they get what they're after."

"Which means we need to tie up all loose ends," King said, "Including Ghost."

I thought about what Ghost had said when I visited him with Nitro. "You need to go see him, King. And I think you're going to have to find a way to make peace with him. At least enough so that he has no reason to talk."

King thought about that for a moment. "Fuck," he muttered. "The last fucking thing I want to do is see that asshole. Let alone offer him any-fucking-thing."

"What the hell would be enough for him to shut his mouth?" Hyde asked.

King's gaze met Hyde's. "I know what it is. But do I want to do it is the question."

King's phone rang then, distracting him from discussing Ghost any further. "Jesus Christ, this fucking woman never stops calling me," he said as he checked caller ID.

"Jen?" I asked. I'd been checking in with her, and she still hadn't seen or heard from him since I mentioned it to him on Thursday.

He put the phone to his ear. When he spoke, his voice was deathly calm. "I'm coming home tonight. I hope to fuck that baby is still kicking." He listened to her and then said, "Stop talking, Jen. Get your shit together and be ready to listen to what I have to say when I get there. And I swear to fucking God, if you push me, it'll be the end of everything."

After he ended the call and shoved his phone in his pocket, he glanced at the both of us, eyes wild, and barked, "First, we get this shit done with Bones. Then, we organise a visit with Ghost. After that, I need to sink my dick into some sweet pussy so I'm calm enough to go home and deal with Jen's shit."

Hyde and I watched for a moment as he stalked away from us. "Fucking hell," Hyde murmured, "that bitch has him so fucking wired that even I'm concerned for her safety."

I hadn't seen King this crazed in a long time and hoped like hell Jen didn't fuck with him anymore than she already had. The club needed his attention, and we hadn't fully had it this week. Surprisingly, Hyde had stepped up when we needed him and had directed our activities during the week while King drank and screwed his way through it. The tension between the two of them had eased somewhat because of this, so at least something good had come from this whole fuck-up.

Hyde and I followed King, and ten minutes later, we were sitting with Bones in the back of a seedy bar listening to him tell us what he'd heard around the traps about Marx.

Bones leaned forward and lowered his voice, "Word is, someone's out to wipe Storm off the map." His gaze zeroed in on King, and he lifted his chin at him. "Someone with a grudge against you."

Hyde grunted. "Well, fuck, that narrows it down."

He was right; the list that held King's enemies was long.

"Who'd you hear this off?" King asked.

Bones rested back against his seat and spread his arms along the couch. Shaking his head, he said, "Nah, I'm not giving you that, but I will tell you that it's come from a few sources, and their info is usually reliable as fuck."

The scowl on King's face would usually scare most people into giving him what he wanted, but Bones had been dealing with us for long enough that he wasn't as affected anymore. That, and the fact King had gone a little soft on him lately. King's guilt over what happened to Nitro with his uncle mixed with the fact it was Bones who helped save him, led to King going easy on him since then.

"So what the fuck has this got to do with Marx?" King demanded. "Marx is tied up with whoever wants us gone? And they're trying to get to us through our drug trade? That doesn't make sense. We deal far and wide with the coke. They'd struggle to take that from us."

"Plus we have other shit going on that gives us a nice income," Hyde threw in. "There's never a shortage of assholes asking for our help and paying us well for it."

My thoughts were the same as Hyde's. Storm was often called in to clean up the messes that people made. We were the cleaners you called when you wanted to ensure no one ever found out what you'd done. And so long as you had the cash, we took the job on.

Bones shrugged. "I don't know. I'm just telling you what I've heard." Standing, he said, "I've gotta get back to work. I'll call if I hear anything else."

King rested his back against the couch and scrubbed his face.

When he didn't say anything, Hyde said, "You think this is Gambarro?"

King stared into space for a few moments, deep in thought, before glancing at Hyde. "No. This doesn't feel like Gambarro."

"Why?" Hyde asked.

"This feels like it's been set up for a while. The shit with Gambarro isn't that old. It only began because of Kick and what we did for him. My gut's telling me this is bigger than that."

"So we need a list of names of everyone with a grudge against you, and we start working through that list until we figure this shit out," I said.

King blew out a frustrated breath. "Fuck."

The meeting with Bones was meant to shed some light for us and help us nail down Marx and his plans. Instead, it only gave us a fuckload more questions and no answers.

Chapter Twenty-One

Hailee

I raised my glass and clinked it with Leona's. "Thank fuck this week is almost over," I said before taking a long sip of my cocktail.

Saturday night had finally come around, and after a long day of giving massages, I was ready to let my hair down and dance all night.

Leona hit me with a smile as she sipped her Coke. She was still hoping like crazy that her hubby knocked her up the previous night, so she wasn't on the hard stuff. "You deserve that drink after living through that dinner with your mother."

"Damn, girl, you have the best smile," I said, engrossed in that rather than what she'd said about my mother. Truth be told, I didn't want to think about my mother.

A woman's voice sounded from behind us, breaking into out conversation. "Now that's the kind of chick you wanna keep close. Someone who isn't afraid to give out a compliment to her friends."

I turned and found Monroe behind me. "Oh, God, you're not gonna try and get me to drink another Jägerbomb with you, are you?"

She moved next to us at the bar and placed her purse on the counter. With a quick wave of her hand, she said, "You don't know what you're missing." She watched as I took another long sip of my drink. "Bad day, honey?"

"No, today was good. It was the week that was off."

"Is your band playing tonight?"

"No. I've been sick this week, so we cancelled the couple of gigs we had booked."

Her eyes twinkled. "You really should let me buy you a Jägerbomb. Guaranteed to kill off any lasting germs."

I couldn't help but laugh. "You love that shit, don't you?"

Doug leant across the counter at that point. He'd caught the last bit of our conversation. "She loves that shit almost as much as she loves pierced dicks."

Leona almost choked on her drink. Her eyes widened a little as she said, "Oh, wow… goodness." She wasn't a prude, but she certainly wasn't as adventurous as some in the bedroom.

"Oh, honey," Monroe said, eyeing Leona, "you really should try a pierced cock at least once in your life. I finally found one recently and let me tell you, best sex I've ever had."

"Uh, I'm married," Leona said a little hesitantly.

"You reckon he'd get it pierced for you?" Monroe asked, deadly serious.

Leona's eyes bulged. "God, no. I'm not sure what Jerry would do if I even mentioned it."

Doug placed a Jägerbomb on the counter for Monroe and glanced at Leona. "Babe, just ignore Monroe. She could talk about pierced dicks all day every day, and thinks every man should have one."

I grinned at him. "What do you think, Doug? Would you get a piercing?"

His eyes met mine and he hit me with that slow, sexy smile of his before saying, "What makes you think I don't already?"

Monroe almost spat out her drink. "Fuck, dude, have you been holding out on me?"

Pushing off from the bar, he said, "You'll never know."

Leona sipped her Coke and said, "I think he likes you, Hailee." She'd never been to this pub with me before, so she didn't know our history.

Monroe skulled her drink before saying, "Oh, he does, honey. I've seen the way he looks at her. But then again, Doug's a flirt from way back."

I shrugged. "We nearly slept together once. It was best that it didn't happen."

Arms circled my waist, and warm breath hit my neck as a deep voice rumbled in my ear, "Who did you nearly fuck once? And should I be keeping my eye on him?"

My belly instantly fluttered and my legs swayed. Turning, I looked up at Devil, taking in the dark desire burning in his gaze. "Hello," I murmured, unable to form more words because he had me all tongue-tied.

His gaze pierced me. "You didn't answer my question. Who did you nearly fuck?"

Oh, God, he was jealous. The way he held me like he never wanted to let me go, the burn in his eyes, and the way he demanded an answer, all screamed his jealousy.

Placing my hands against his chest, I said, "Do you really want to know? Or should we just take this home and I'll show you that you're the only man I'm into these days?"

He thought about that for a moment. Shaking his head, he forced out, "I don't want to know."

Taking hold of my hand, he dragged me away from the girls, through the Saturday night crowd and to a corner table in the pub. By the time he sat down and pulled me onto his lap so I straddled him, my breaths were coming hard and fast.

"Fuck, De—"

He cut me off when he pulled my lips to his and kissed me. It was our roughest kiss yet, and it erased all thoughts from my mind except for those about him.

When he ended the kiss, my heart was almost beating outside my chest. "What was that about?" I asked, wondering what the hell had gotten into him.

He moved his hands to my thighs and ran them up my legs and under my dress. "Fuck if I know, darlin'. Jealousy isn't usually a problem of mine, but the thought of another man with you just about sent me fucking crazy."

I didn't love jealousy and was glad it wasn't the norm for him, but I adored what I heard in his voice. The fact he wanted me so much and didn't want to share me made me feel special. No one had ever made me feel that wanted.

Reaching for his jeans, I popped the button and slid the zip down. My fingers worked fast, and I soon had my hand wrapped around his dick.

He watched as I stroked him, his eyes closing for a brief moment before opening again and meeting my gaze. "You gonna give me a hand job in public?"

Lust sizzled along my skin. Bending so my mouth was next to his ear, I said, "No, I'm going to fuck you in public." His sharp intake of breath made my pussy clench. As far as I was concerned, I couldn't get him inside me fast enough. The pub was packed that night, and noisy as hell. We sat in the darkened corner, and I figured most people were too busy doing their own thing to even realise what we were doing.

He ran his hands up my back as our eyes met again. "You're going to fuck me here on this chair for everyone to see?" Disbelief coated his words.

I continued pumping his cock, loving the hiss that escaped his lips. "You should stop doubting me and start getting on board with this. I'm wearing a dress and no underwear. It's the perfect opp—"

"Fuck," he rasped as he ran his hands further under my dress to reach for my ass. When he realised I wasn't lying about wearing no panties, he said, "I'm on fucking board. Never let it be said I ever doubted my woman."

I grinned as I pressed my mouth to his. Half kissing him, I said, "I like it when you call me your woman."

He gripped my ass cheeks. "And I like it when you show me your dirty side like this. There should be more sex in public as far as I'm concerned."

"I've never fucked a man in public before you."

"Baby," he growled, "I never wanna hear those words or any words like them out of that mouth again. The less I have to think about you with another man, the fucking better."

I melted against him. "I like it when you call me baby, too."

"So we've established I should call you my woman and baby a lot fucking more, especially if I wanna get fucked in public. Can we move to the part of this night where my dick finally gets inside you?"

"Such a way with words," I murmured as I positioned my pussy over his dick, making sure my dress covered everything.

"Fuck," he groaned as I sank down on him. His hands left my ass so he could hold my hips, and he bent his head so he could suck my neck.

I held his biceps as I fucked him, my fingers digging into his skin while my pleasure built. This whole fucking-in-public thing was something I could do a whole lot more of. I'd been hesitant when we'd had sex in the staff room weeks ago, but the thrill of it all made me want more.

"Jesus, Hailee, I want to bend you over this fucking table and pound my fucking dick into you while everyone watches," he rasped.

My breaths quickened. I was coming out of my skin, unsure of how much more I could take. "I'm not sure I won't scream when I come," I panted, my pussy pulsing as I fought my release.

I was so close.

So fucking close.

I never wanted it to end, though. Devil felt too good inside me like this.

He bit my neck and then licked a line along my skin until he met my mouth. "Scream, darlin'. I don't give a fuck if everyone knows you're riding my dick."

"Fuck," I moaned as I dug my fingers into his arms again. "You are so fucking dirty."

He'd been letting me take the lead, but suddenly he stole it back. Gripping my hips, he moved me up and down on him while thrusting his dick in hard. Anyone who was watching would know what we were doing.

His mouth found mine, consuming me with a savage kiss. Between that and him fucking me the way he was, my orgasm shattered through me. I tried like hell to slow it, but Devil was a force that couldn't be stopped. He wanted to make me come. And I fucking came.

I buried my scream in his neck, sucking him hard while I orgasmed.

When we were done, his eyes found mine. "I'll never doubt you again, baby."

I kissed him one last time. "Stop calling me baby, or else I'm gonna wanna go again right here, right now."

His lips spread out in a huge-ass grin and his arms wrapped around me. "You're gonna get us kicked out of this joint, *baby*."

I rested my forehead against his. “You’re killing me here.”

He tightened his hold on me. “Woman, you killed me the first fucking night I met you.”

***

I stared at my grandmother with wide eyes. “Uh, you do realise this could all go to hell, don’t you?”

She flicked her wrist at me as if to say, “Hush, child.” She then said, “Aaron needs to understand you’re serious about Dominic. Lunch together will do them good.”

“I get where you’re coming from, but I think a little more time apart might help him come to terms with our relationship. Let him see how strong we grow as time goes on.”

She’d just informed me that she’d invited Aaron to lunch at our home that day, after she’d already invited Devil. Aaron had been loud in his disapproval of Devil, and I didn’t see him backing down anytime soon. But Gran always had her own views on things, and she disagreed with me on this.

The sound of someone at the front door interrupted us. A moment later, Aaron entered the kitchen, flowers in hand. Passing them to Gran, he pressed a kiss to her forehead. “Lunch smells good.”

“She’s made your favourite. I’m pretty sure it’s to bribe you into being nice.”

His eyes narrowed at me. “Are you going to give me bad news or something?”

“Something like that,” I muttered.

“Hailee,” he said in a warning tone. “What’s going on?”

A knock on the front door saved me, and I ignored his question to go answer it.

Devil's eyes trailed down my body as I walked towards him. The screen door was the only thing separating us, and I was fairly sure by the glint I saw in his eyes that it was possibly the only thing stopping him putting his hands all over me.

I didn't open the door straight away. Staring at him through it, I said, "I'm not sure you'll want to come in."

He frowned. "Why not?"

I sighed, frustrated at my grandmother, but more so with Aaron for making things difficult. "Aaron's here. Gran invited him because she thinks you two need time to get to know each other."

He stepped forward, a look of determination on his face. "Open the door, Hailee."

I hesitated. "Are you sure?"

"Open it. No one's stopping me from seeing you. Not even your brother." His voice was forceful, and while I loved his stubbornness, I also feared the fireworks that could erupt when he and my brother were in the same room.

Reluctantly, I let him in. His hands moved straight to my waist so he could pull me close for a kiss.

"What the fuck is he doing here?" Aaron bellowed from the other end of the hallway. As he stalked our way, I felt Devil's body tense, and I silently prayed for peace between these two.

My grandmother appeared in the hallway. "*I* invited him." She took the Gran tone she'd liked to use when chastising us as kids.

Aaron slowed, shock registering on his features. Turning back to face her, he said, "You support this relationship?"

She nodded. "Yes."

"You do know he's a biker, right? And that his club is tied up in some bad shit."

"Fuck," Devil swore under his breath.

I held him next to me when I sensed he was about to move towards Aaron. Anger vibrated off both of them, scaring me a little. I hoped Gran knew what she was doing.

"I know all of that, Aaron, but I also know that Dominic is the best man I've ever seen with my granddaughter. Hailee's smiling like I've never seen her smile, and confident in a way she's never been. He makes her happy. And as far as him being a biker, since when do we judge people? I thought I helped raise you to be better than that."

"You would judge bikers the same way I do if you were in the line of work I'm in."

Gran's voice softened a little when she said, "And you've been perfect your entire life, then? Never done something you weren't proud of?"

Aaron had turned to look at Devil right before she said that, and he froze at her questions. His face paled, and instead of answering her, he stalked back into the kitchen.

"Way to go, Gran," I whispered.

"She sure has a way of getting her point across," Devil said softly enough so only I heard him.

I looked up at him. Touching his cheek, I said, "Okay, you good to do this? I don't think it's gonna be fun."

He nodded. "Nothing worth anything in life is easy, darlin'."

He led me into the kitchen while I held my breath a little.

God, please don't let this turn to shit.

Chapter Twenty-Two

Devil

Bronze and I managed to make it through most of dinner without trying to take each other's heads off. And then Hailee's asshole neighbour happened.

Jean had just served dessert, and I'd taken my first bite of the best pavlova I'd ever tasted when the fight next door started.

"God, does he ever lay off her?" Hailee muttered, pushing her chair back to stand.

Bronze quickly stood, too. "Sit back down, Hailee. I'll go over and see what's happening."

Screams came from the house next door. The kind that signaled a woman was terrified for her safety. It was the first time I'd heard them since hanging out at Hailee's home.

I pushed my chair out. "I'll come with you."

Bronze scowled. "I'll go on my own."

"You should both go," Jean said. "He's been drinking today, Aaron. You might need the help this time."

The guy sounded like a real piece of work.

I followed Bronze outside and across the yard to the neighbour's house. We didn't exchange words until we reached the front door. The screams had stopped, so Bronze took a moment to say, "You think you can control your urge to punch him? Because the last fucking thing I need here is you letting loose and him filing a report against us."

My fists clenched by my side. Lifting my chin at the door, I said, "Let's just get this shit over with so we finish lunch and then you can go home."

"*I* can go home? You think you're staying or something?"

"Jesus, Bronze—"

A scream from inside drew our attention back to the job at hand, and Bronze banged hard on the front door. "Police! Open up!"

Silence.

And then the front door was yanked open and a pissed off guy stood glaring at us. "Yeah?"

Bronze pushed his way inside, and I followed behind while the asshole protested after slamming the door shut.

We found a woman cowering in the corner of the kitchen with a bloody nose and bruises on her face. Bronze crouched next to her. "He hit you again, Maria?"

She stared at him with fearful eyes that darted from Bronze to the asshole who'd hit her. She didn't appear to want to tell Bronze what had happened, and when the asshole started yelling at us, she ducked her head and covered it with her hands.

"We don't fucking need your help," the asshole yelled.

Bronze stood. "Yeah, see I'm thinking you do. Just like every other fucking time you get your drink on and lose your shit with her."

The asshole snarled. "What you need to do is mind your own damn business. She's fine, and I just want to watch the fucking television in peace without any of you fucking interrupting me."

My carefully controlled temper snapped, and I stepped forward to get in the guy's face. "She interrupt your peace, did she, asshole? Is that why you punched the fuck out of her?"

His eyes glinted with hate. "Yeah, matter of fact, she did. What's it to you?"

Without a second thought, I swung my fist straight into his face, knocking him flat on his ass on the hard tiles of the kitchen.

"Fucking hell, Devil, I told you to keep your goddam shit together," Bronze roared.

I ignored him and stepped over the guy so I could grab his shirt and reef him up. Once I had him standing, I spun him around and slammed him hard against the pantry door, taking care to smash his head hard against it. I then punched his face again. Twice. When he hit the floor for the second time, I crouched down next to him and said, "That's what it is to me, motherfucker. I'm practically living next door to you now. If I so much as *think* you're taking to her with your fists, I'll be over here. And that pain you're feeling now? It's fucking nothing compared to what you'll get off me next time."

I left him and stalked outside, barely able to stomach being inside his house. When I was almost back to Hailee's front door, I stopped and bent, resting my hands on my knees. Taking some long deep breaths, I attempted to get myself under control. I didn't want to go inside while in this state of anger.

"What the fuck was that shit?" Bronze yelled.

"I was just doing what you can't," I snapped. "And besides, that kind of cunt only responds to fists and threats. He's hardly gonna listen to anything you have to say."

Hailee ran outside, her face and body displaying the stress I heard in her words when she asked, "Did everything go okay?"

Ignoring her, Bronze looked at me and said, "As far as you practically living here, you know where I stand on that, so I suggest you reassess that statement."

He left us alone, stalking inside.

Hailee looked up at me with a frown. "What did he mean by that?"

Fuck.

I hadn't told her how I knew her brother, and I sure as fuck hadn't told her about his ultimatum. I wasn't about to, either.

Snaking my arm around her waist, I said, "Nothing, darlin'. We'll sort our shit out soon."

Shaking her head, she said, "Devil, don't lie to me. I know he's got a problem with me dating you. Has he said something to you about it?"

"He's made it clear he doesn't want us to date, yes. But, Hailee"—I strengthened my hold on her—"I'm not walking away, okay? Your brother will have to either come around or learn to live with us being together."

She nodded like she believed me, but I saw the doubt in her eyes. I resolved to do whatever it took to get Bronze on side. No fucking way was he coming between me and the woman I wanted by my side.

***

Monday rolled around, and so did Storm's problems.

"Got a job for you and Hyde," King said, coming out of his office when I hit the clubhouse first thing. He looked as tired as I felt.

"What?" I said as I yawned.

His forehead creased with a frown. "You get any sleep last night, Devil?"

"Some." Hailee had kept me up half the night so I couldn't complain. But a later alarm would have been appreciated. She always set her alarm for 6:00 fucking a.m. to do her meditation. I needed to find a way to still get as much sex in as we did, but with more sleep. Possibly getting her naked much fucking earlier would do it, but then again, we'd probably just fuck for longer and still not get much sleep.

"Devil! Are you fucking hearing a word I'm saying?"

I blinked and yawned again. "No, but I was wondering how you went with Jen on Saturday night? Did you go home and talk to her?"

"Yeah, she's sorted."

"As in?" It felt like I cared more about her than he did at this point, and that was saying something because I cared almost nothing for her.

"Fuck, Devil, what is this? Monday fucking sharing circle?" He rubbed the back of his neck. "I told her she can stay with me while she's pregnant and then until she finds her feet. After that, I want her gone. Now, can we please get back to club shit?"

"What's on for today?" I was more than happy to get back to club shit.

"I need you and Hyde to collect cash off a few assholes today."

"Where's Kick?" It was usually his job to do collections.

"Evie's in hospital. They're having some complications with the pregnancy, so I've told him to take whatever time he needs with her."

I nodded. "Is Hyde in already?"

"Yeah." At my stunned expression, he said, "Surprised the fuck outta me, too, brother."

After months of Hyde being off the rails with his moods, and being MIA more often than not, he'd finally gotten his shit together over the last couple of weeks and was back to putting the club first.

"You ready to go?" Hyde joined us, no sign of his usual morning grumpiness at all.

"Be back by lunch. Devil, you're with me for my visit with Ghost this afternoon," King said.

As we walked out to our bikes, I wondered what the hell had happened with Hyde to change his mood so drastically. In the end, I decided it had to be pussy. I couldn't think of anything else that would change his asshole ways in such a short amount of time.

***

I glared at the motherfucker giving us the fucking run around. My mood had turned foul as the morning progressed, and no fucking way did I have the patience to deal with his shit. On top of that, the heat had grown unbearable. We were dealing with fucking forty-plus degree heat, and we were doing that inside this motherfucker's tiny tin shed of a fucking house.

"Look," I snapped, "have you got the cash or fucking not?"

He grimaced, and I knew we weren't going to get very far, very fucking fast. "Well, I do, but it—"

Hyde had been patient up until that point, again surprising me, but he'd found his breaking point, too. Stepping forward, he scrunched a handful of the guy's shirt in his hand. "There's no room for any buts in all this, asshole. If the next words out of your mouth aren't that you've got the cash, you're gonna meet my fists."

The guy continued to shake his head and plead his case. "I can bring it to you in a few days."

Hyde grunted as he let the guy's shirt go and punched him hard in the face. His mouth spread out in a satisfied expression as he watched the asshole slump to the ground.

Glancing at me, he said, "Best part of the fucking day so far."

"We need to hurry this along, Hyde. The heat in here is fucked."

Hyde looked back at the guy. "You want a finger or a whole hand, Devil?"

The guy's eyes just about popped out of his head. "What?"

Hyde pulled out his knife and ran it down the asshole's face. "You didn't think we'd leave empty-handed, did you? We have to take something back to our president, and if it's not cash, a body part will do for now."

Right as the guy was about to get into it with us, shots rang out and bullets sprayed the house, smashing through the front windows.

Hyde and I ran towards the front door, ducking to avoid being shot. A car had screeched to a stop outside, and as we shot at it, the driver slammed his foot to the floor and took off.

"Forget the asshole inside," Hyde yelled. "I wanna know who the fuck that was."

I agreed with him, and a couple of minutes later, we were in pursuit on our bikes. Adrenaline spiked in my veins. Fucking getting shot at wasn't something I appreciated, and the urge to deliver payback roared so loudly I felt like it would bleed out of me.

Weaving in and out of traffic, we quickly caught up to the car. Hot, smoggy wind whipped around me while horns blared and brakes squealed. Fury at having to deal with this shit crashed into the irritation the fucking heat had caused me. When I got my hands on these motherfuckers, they would regret aiming their guns at us.

From what I could work out, there were two men in the car. Hyde was ahead of me and signaled for me to take the driver side while he took the passenger side. I sped up to do as he'd indicated, but as we approached, the car abruptly turned right into a side street, almost causing me to come off my bike.

Fuck.

We adjusted course and followed them down a narrow street with bends all through it that tested any patience I had left.

Taking advantage of this road having little traffic, the guy in the passenger side stuck his head out the window and shot at us.

Motherfucker.

I gripped the bike harder while doing my best to avoid getting fucking killed while also navigating around parked cars.

The end of the street came into view, and I watched as the car took the corner too sharply. It smashed into an oncoming car, and I figured we would get the chance to find out who we were dealing with. *And the opportunity for vengeance.* Yet as we drew closer, the fuckhead driver revved the engine and sped away from the crash scene.

We followed as best we could, but the traffic was a fucking shitfight, making it difficult for us to weave in and out. Lunchtime foot traffic didn't help either, slowing us, too. The dirty white car we followed soon became a speck in the distance. We didn't give up easily, but when we found ourselves stuck at a red light in gridlocked traffic in the middle of Sydney, I knew we were done. I also knew that when we finally did figure out who tried to kill us, I'd take great fucking pleasure in ripping their balls off and shoving them down their bastard throats. Fuckers. No one messed with Storm.

Once we got through the city and out of the heavy traffic, I followed Hyde's lead and pulled over to the side of the road.

Ripping his helmet off, he muttered, "I've got no fucking idea who that was. You?"

I shook my head. "No, but we've got a number plate we can run. I doubt it'll do us any good, but it's worth a shot."

"I'll get onto that while you head out to see Ghost. I'm gonna make it my fucking mission to find out who those motherfuckers were."

***

Ghost's eyes held more suspicion than I'd ever seen in any person when he faced King and me that afternoon. He refused to sit. Rather, he stood and watched us with his arms folded across his chest.

King's lips curled up in annoyance. "For fuck's sake, sit, Ghost," he barked.

Ghost's body tensed. If we hadn't been in a prison with guards' eyes on us, I was fairly sure he'd take a swing at King. "I stopped listening to you a long fucking time ago. I'm hardly gonna start again."

"You will when you hear what I've got to say."

A flicker of interest flared in Ghost's eyes. He attempted to hide it, but if I'd seen it, King wouldn't have missed it. "How about you spit it out and then I'll decide whether I sit or not?"

King's hands landed on the table, and he shot out of his seat. In a low, menacing voice, he said, "How about you fucking sit or else I'll make sure your stay in this shithole is extended."

I had no doubt he would, too. King had that kind of power, and if someone pissed him off he didn't hesitate to use it.

Ghost scowled, but he sat.

King followed suit before saying, "You seen the feds again?"

Ghost's stubborn side kicked in. "I'm not answering that until I know what's on the table."

King leant forward and dropped his voice to speak quietly. "Your parole is coming up."

Ghost took in the full meaning of what King meant and blew out a pissed off breath. "You're a fucking cunt, King."

"Yeah, that might be, but I do what I do for the club." He stopped for a moment before adding, "Except when an asshole tries to step in on my territory. The shit I do to him for that is solely for my benefit." Fuck, we were going to dredge up the Jen shit from years ago.

"Jesus, are you ever gonna let that go? I was fucking drunk. And Jen wasn't into it, anyway."

King's eyes darkened as he shook his head. "I'm not talking about Jen."

I sat up straighter and looked at King. This was news to me.

Ghost stared at King for a long silent few moments, recognition all over his face. He knew what King was talking about. "Fuck, man, that was a long fucking time ago. I was young and dumb as shit. And so was she."

King's body snapped back as anger flooded his face. Violent, raging, lethal anger. "Don't ever fucking talk about her like that again."

I blinked. I'd seen King in a murderous rage many times, but this… this was off the fucking charts. The venom laced through his words revealed the level of hatred he had for Ghost. If I were sitting on the other side of the table being asked if I wanted parole, I'd say fuck no. Because the minute Ghost got out, he'd need to take cover from King. And there weren't many places in this country that anyone could be safe from my president. His reach was that far and wide.

Ghost's face whitened. "Look, Ivy was—"

King punched the table. "Don't fucking say her name!"

"Jesus, King," I muttered, eyeing the guard watching us. "You're drawing attention."

He ignored me. "You thought I'd never find out, Ghost? What I can't figure out is why you even thought Ivy would be into you? And don't try to feed me some bullshit about her saying yes to you. Jen told me everything you told her about that day."

Ghost looked down at his hands resting on the table. He didn't answer King straight away, and I wondered where this would all end up. I joined the club a long time after Ivy left, so I didn't know what had gone on. But I'd heard the stories about the love King had for her. Apparently when she'd left, it had ripped him apart, and he'd spent years getting over her. I was beginning to think he'd never gotten over her, because I'd never seen him like this over Jen or any other woman.

When Ghost finally looked back up at King, the fight had gone out of him. I couldn't be sure, but I thought I saw guilt flash in his eyes when he spoke. "I was twenty-three then, King, and all I ever seemed to do was fuck shit up. I was drunk every damn day, and half the time I had no idea what I was doing."

"So that makes it okay to try and fuck someone else's woman? The thing is, Ghost, it wasn't just my woman you tried it on with. You screwed anyone who stepped on your path. And because of the power you had in the club, you got away with it. Over and fucking over."

We all sat in silence after that. Ghost had nothing to come back with, and it seemed that King had said all he would on the subject.

Finally, King stood and said, "You keep your mouth shut when the feds visit and move your sister back home so I know where she is, and I'll help push your parole through. You don't do any of those things, and we're done for good. I'll happily ensure you rot in this hellhole."

On our way out to our bikes, after King had secured Ghost's agreement, I said, "You didn't strip him of VP because of Jen, did you?"

King slowed, his eyes meeting mine. "No." His gaze drifted off somewhere behind me for a beat, before coming back to me.

"I didn't fight hard enough for Ivy back then. The minute I could, I fucking did."

I didn't understand his meaning, but that was the thing with King—most people often didn't. He talked in riddles half the time, and his mind sometimes worked in ways that made no sense to me. But if you needed someone on your side who was loyal as fuck, King was your man. I couldn't even begin to imagine a time when he wouldn't fight hard for someone he cared about, and I wondered what had gone on back then for that to have happened.

Chapter Twenty-Three

Hailee

I pulled my car into the driveway and killed the engine. Rummaging in my handbag, I found what I was looking for at the very bottom. Pulling a tissue from the packet, I wiped the tears from my eyes.

No one needed to see me like this.

It had been the Monday from hell, and I'd cancelled all plans for the night, including our usual Monday performance at Flirt. I'd also texted Devil to say I was going home to bed. I just wanted to curl into a ball and forget the world for the night.

My phone buzzed with a text on the seat beside me.

Dylan: You need me to go see that bitch and give her a piece of my mind?

Me: Did Leona tell you what happened?

I hadn't told a soul. The only ones who knew were my workmates, who'd witnessed my meltdown.

The phone rang, and I answered it with a sigh. "I'm okay, Dylan. Really. I'm sorry I cancelled tonight's gig, but I just don't have it in me to smile and sing."

"Babe, I couldn't give a fuck about the gig. Do you want me to come over? You could give me a massage, and I could tell you what a bitch Rachel is."

He never failed to make me laugh, even when I was down for the count. "I'm gonna have to find you a girlfriend who knows how to massage, just so you quit begging me."

"Could be a good idea. I'm not thinking your boyfriend would be happy if your hands were always on me."

"Yeah, you might be on to something there."

"Okay, so I'm going to come over. No massage required."

The rumble of a bike distracted me, and I glanced out the window of the car to see Devil pulling his bike in behind me.

"No, don't come over. Devil's just turned up." I softened my voice when I added, "But thank you. Love you, Dylan."

"Love you, too, babe. I'll call you tomorrow to make sure you're okay."

I ended the call and threw my phone in my bag. Exiting the car, I smiled at Devil as he approached.

"Fuck, darlin', you look like hell." Concern etched lines into his face as he reached for me.

I placed my hand in his and allowed him to pull me close. He was right—my face was black with wet mascara from all the tears I'd cried on my way home from work. "Thanks, it's always good when your boyfriend tells you that you look like shit."

He ignored my sarcasm. "Leona called and told me you got into it with Rachel."

My eyes held his. "So you just dropped everything and came straight over?" I asked softly, my heart beating rapidly at that thought.

"Yeah." He said it like I'd just asked the dumbest question ever. Like, *of course* he would drop everything and come to me.

I reached up to run my fingers lightly over his lips. "You better be careful, Dominic Ford, because I might just be falling in love with you."

He took hold of my hand. "I'll never be careful if that's what it'll get me."

I moved so my body was flush against his and pulled his mouth to mine. Before I kissed him, I said, "Only you could show up here, when I feel the way I do, and make me feel like life is so fucking good."

"What happened with Rachel?"

"She gave me a choice—my job or my charity work. We argued over it for a bit, and then I told her to shove her fucking job. I still don't know for sure my investor is going ahead, and I really can't afford to be out of work, but I can't stay there another day." I felt ill over my decision, but at the same time, I felt deep in my bones that it was the right choice. At this point, I was putting my trust in the universe for it to all work out okay.

Devil nodded and pressed his lips to mine. His kiss was gentle, loving. He always seemed to know just what I needed. When he ended the kiss, he said, "You made the right choice, darlin'. I've watched you deal with her shit for weeks now, and that bitch doesn't deserve you. We'll get through this. It'll all work out."

I smiled up at him. "*We'll?*" My question was almost a whisper. I was hesitant to fully embrace what I thought he meant by that word, but God, I wanted to.

"Yes, *we*," he said with conviction, making this whole shitty day so much better.

I hooked a hand around his neck while also sliding a leg around him so I could lift myself into his arms. "Okay, so I'm thinking we should have dinner here with Gran tonight—she's making my favourite—and then you should take me back to your place so you can fuck me in ways that will make me scream so loudly it might cause the roof to cave in."

He lifted a brow. “You don’t want me to do that to you here?”

I grinned. “Smart-ass.” Gran didn’t need to hear me calling out his name over and over.

“What’s your favourite dinner?”

“Sticky pork spare ribs.” My mouth watered just thinking about them. “God, you are going to love them. Gran makes them the best I’ve ever had.”

“I’ll have to get that recipe off her if it makes you this fucking horny.”

I tightened my arms around his neck. “Careful,” I warned. “I’m falling.” Truth be told, I’d already fallen for him. Hard.

“I’m counting on it, baby.”

At the sound of a car pulling up, he turned, and I saw Aaron parking on the street in front of the house. He stalked our way, his face an angry mask.

“We’re done, Devil!”

Devil put me down and stepped forward to meet Aaron, his shoulders tense.

Aaron’s eyes met mine. “Go inside, Hailee. This is between us.”

I straightened. “No, anything you’ve got to say to Devil, you say to me, too.”

He shook his head and swore under his breath before turning back to face Devil. “I’ve just chased up that number plate from today. Those guys are tied to Marx.” His voice hardened as he added, “They’re the kind of guys who don’t fucking mess around, Devil. They’ll be back.”

“And when they come, we’ll be ready for them.” Devil’s tone was just as hard.

“Exactly how do you see that playing out? Because from where I stand, I see my sister being put right in the middle of danger here." He jabbed his finger in the air at Devil. "And that is the reason why I told you to walk away."

I frowned. "Wait. You two know each other?" A vague memory of the day we met in the back of Aaron's car drifted into my mind, and I realised that they must have known each other back then. I wasn't sure why I hadn't connected the dots.

"Yeah," Aaron said, "we do."

My mind was a jumbled mess of thoughts. I looked at Devil. "Why is he running plates for you?"

Devil scrubbed a hand over his face. "Fuck, it's complicated, Hailee."

My eyes widened, and I turned to Aaron. "You're running plates to give Storm information, aren't you?" The sinking feeling I had in my stomach made me feel ill.

"Yes," Aaron admitted, and everything I knew about my brother was suddenly muddy.

He's a dirty cop.

"How long have you been dirty?" I demanded, as I wondered what else I didn't know about him.

"That's not important. What *is* important is that you stay away from Storm."

He reached for me, but I pulled my arm away. "I don't need to stay away from anyone, Aaron. All I need, right now, is for you to answer my question. How long?"

"Hailee—"

"No!" I yelled, not wanting to hear his excuses. "You stood there the other day and judged bikers as if you were better than them. I have no issues with bikers. What I have an issue with is someone pretending to be something they're not, and then lording that over others." I took a step away. "I need a moment to get my thoughts together."

With that, I left them to it and stalked inside. I needed a quiet space to think. I was so damn disappointed in Aaron. I loved him unconditionally, but sometimes he managed to do shit I really didn't agree with or understand. I hated that he'd treated Devil so badly, acting as if he were the better man because he was a cop. I believed everyone was equal and found it hard to fathom people who didn't think the same way. I also found it really fucking difficult to like people who discriminated against others.

Damn you, Aaron.

I raked my fingers through my hair as I worked hard to reconcile my feelings towards my brother.

"Hailee," Gran said, a frown on her face as she found me sitting alone in the lounge room. "What's wrong?"

"I just need a moment, Gran, and then I'll tell you." I had to get my thoughts under control, otherwise I'd be shooting my mouth off and potentially say things I'd later regret. "Can you please go and make sure Aaron and Devil aren't trying to kill each other out the front?" They'd been projecting that vibe when I left them. I hoped they could both be man enough not to act on it.

She nodded and did as I asked, leaving me alone again. I'd been sitting there for a good five minutes or so when I heard shouting from the front yard.

Aaron's voice.

I made my way out there again, horrified to find them fighting. Punches flew thick and fast. Both of them seemed determined to inflict as much pain on the other as possible. My own anger flared while I watched them. Why couldn't the two men in my life find a way to get along? "Gran! Why are you just standing there doing nothing?"

She grabbed my arm as I tried to push past her to go to them. "Leave them be, baby girl."

I spun around to face her, just as horrified at her response. "*Really*? You want us to just stand here and watch as they try to kill each other?" My heart rate sped up at that thought. I couldn't do it. I wouldn't.

"You're being dramatic, child. This is what men do. I don't understand it either, but it seems to work for them. Maybe after they get it out of their systems, they'll be able to move forward and leave each other alone."

Confusion crashed all around me.

Was she right?

Would this actually fix anything?

In the end, I realised one thing—me trying to get in the middle of them would be a waste of time. They were both hell-bent on seeing this fight to the very end. So, I stood with my grandmother and watched in horror as they beat each other up. I struggled to take it all in, and often had to turn away. By the time they were finished, they both lay on the front lawn battered and bloodied, and I wasn't sure either could be called the victor.

Chapter Twenty-Four

Devil

I sat outside Bronze's house on my bike early the next morning, contemplating exactly what I would say to him. I'd woken when Hailee did for her meditation, and had gotten ready for the day, intent on getting to Bronze's before he left for the day. Hailee had decided to skip her meditation and had asked me to drop her home on my way out. She knew where I was headed, and seemed concerned that we'd get into it again, but I assured her we wouldn't.

We needed to fix this shit between us. Our fight the day before had been brutal. I'd been left with swollen eyes I had trouble seeing through, cuts, and bruises. I didn't think anything was broken, but my body hurt like a motherfucker. Bronze had fared about the same. We couldn't keep doing this, and I suspected we would if we didn't get our shit together soon. Either that or he would make good on his threat to walk from the club. That was something I needed to stop from happening.

But what the fuck could I say that he would listen to? He hadn't taken in anything I'd said up to this point, and I really wasn't sure he would at all. Bronze was a stubborn asshole.

"Fuck," I muttered as I closed the distance between my bike and his front door.

I knocked on the door a few times, but he didn't answer. Figuring he could still be asleep, I pulled out my phone and called him. His phone rang, but it sounded like the noise came from just on the other side of the door. If that was the case, why the fuck wasn't he answering it?

"Bronze!" I called out, banging harder on his door this time.

My gut churned with concern when he still didn't answer, so I headed around the back to see if he had any windows open. The unease I felt turned out to be justified when I discovered the back door kicked in. A few moments later, I found him tied up and gagged in his bedroom.

"Jesus fuck," I said as I pulled the gag from his mouth. "What the fuck happened?"

"Three guys happened. They were all wearing balaclavas, though, so I don't know who they were." He grunted while I worked the rope off his hands and feet.

His face was a bloody mess where they'd beaten him, and when he moved from the chair, hunched over, I knew they'd taken to his body, too.

"Fucking assholes will pay for this when I find out who it was," he said.

I followed him down the hallway into the kitchen where he pulled ice from his freezer. "You got some enemies at work who'd do this?" I asked.

Scowling at me, he wrapped the ice and held it to his face. "Clearly I do."

"Don't be a motherfucker. I'm trying to help you here."

"Yeah, well, I don't want your fucking help, Devil."

Ignoring that, I said, "I don't get it. They came here and roughed you up, and that was it? Did they threaten you?"

He hissed as he repositioned the ice on his cheek. "All they said was that I'd screwed them over and I'd pay. They said they'd be back when it was done. Fucked if I know what that meant."

Ice slid down my spine. "Fuck, Bronze." I yanked my phone out of my jeans and dialed Hailee. "Do you think they would have gone after Hailee?"

His jaw clenched, but before he replied, Hailee picked up.

"Hey, you," she said, and I could tell by her voice that she was smiling.

Relief coursed through me. Letting out a long breath, I said, "Thank fuck."

"What's wrong? You sound stressed."

"Darlin', I need you to do something for me, and I need you to do it as fast as possible, okay?"

"Devil, you're scaring me." Her fear bled through the phone, and I cursed silently that she had to go through this.

"Get Jean in the car and drive to the clubhouse. I'll text you the address, and I'll let the boys know you're on the way in case I'm not there by the time you arrive. I'll tell you everything when I get there."

"Shit." Silence, and then—"Okay." Her voice was shaky, but determined. *That's my girl.*

I'm going to hang up now so you can go."

Without waiting for her to say anything else, I ended the call and texted her the address of the clubhouse. I then phoned through to the boys on the gate that she was on her way.

"Thanks."

I glanced up to find Bronze staring at me in what could only be described as begrudging thanks. Nodding, I said, "Yeah."

"I'm gonna head out and try to figure out who it is and what they want," he said.

"Call me if you figure it out. I'll get the boys onto it as well."

As he walked back down the hall towards his bathroom, he said, "This doesn't change anything, Devil."

I was under no illusions. It'd take a lot more than me helping his family for Bronze to come around.

***

I was on my way out of Bronze's place when King called.

"I heard what happened to Bronze," he said. "And I know you're on your way to Hailee at the clubhouse, but I need you on something first."

"What's up?"

"I'm supposed to be meeting Dragon with Hyde and Nitro in half an hour. He's got news for us on Marx. Hyde can't make it, so I need you with us."

"Where?"

"That old warehouse on Jezebel."

I frowned. "Seems like a strange meeting place."

"Yeah, that's why I want you and Nitro there. This whole meet feels off. He's just called it in the last half hour and seemed keen to make it happen straight away."

"Okay, I'm on my way."

I hung up and sped off in the direction of the warehouse he'd mentioned. I had that churning in my gut again. Thank fuck Hailee would be safe at the clubhouse soon.

***

King and Nitro were waiting when I arrived. They stood at the back of the old warehouse that was eerily quiet that morning. It wasn't so much the warehouse that was quiet; it was the street. It was like a fucking ghost town, which was unusual because it was generally filled with traffic.

"What time's Dragon scheduled to be here?" I asked.

King checked the time on his phone. "Now."

Irritation crawled all over me. It came out of nowhere. All I could put it down to was my frustration with being at the warehouse instead of the clubhouse making sure Hailee was safe.

But it manifested as anger towards Hyde. "Where's Hyde? This seems like something he shouldn't miss."

"Yeah, was wondering the same thing," Nitro said.

"He didn't give me an explanation except to say it had something to do with his family," King said.

"His family? I've never heard Hyde mention them before," I said.

"Fuck, Devil," King muttered. "Can we stop fucking going on about Hyde." He was jumpy as shit. In an effort not to piss him off further, I nodded my agreement. But I'd make a point of confronting Hyde about his no-show. I was done with letting his crap slide.

"I think we need to up our club security again," I said. "After what happened yesterday with me and Hyde, it might be a good idea to put more eyes back on our families." We'd pulled back a little over the last couple of months, but unease had settled in my gut. With everything being thrown at the club, I felt like we were being closed in on and that we were losing control. And I'd be damned if Storm went down without a fucking fight.

"I agree," Nitro said.

King nodded and lifted his chin at Nitro. "Take care of it."

Ten minutes passed, in which time King grew increasingly more agitated when Dragon didn't show. After he spent a good chunk of that time pacing and swearing, he called him, but Dragon didn't answer his phone.

"I don't know what his fucking game is, but I'm done with waiting," King snapped. "I've gotta take Jen to the doctor. I'll be back at the clubhouse after that."

"Jesus, I haven't seen him this ugly in a long time," Nitro said as we watched King head to his bike.

"Jen's really fucked him up."

"Yeah, betrayal's a cold bitch."

My phone rang, and I scrambled to answer it, hoping it was Hailee.

"Hey, you," she said, making my fucking day. "We made it to the clubhouse okay, but I forgot to bring Gran's medication with us. Are you able to collect it when you come?"

"Yeah. Where is it?"

"I got it ready to bring, so it's in a bag on the kitchen counter. I can't believe I left without it."

"I'll head over there now. I should be at the clubhouse in about an hour or so. You okay there?"

"Yeah, one of the guys introduced me to Kree. She's lovely. Gran's talking her ear off."

Thank fuck.

Some of the tension in my shoulders eased once I knew she was safe. The rest wouldn't disappear until I saw her for myself.

***

The goddam traffic was a bitch all the way to Hailee's house, and the heat had stripped any patience I had. This all meant I was in a mood by the time I turned into her street.

And then I saw Hailee's home, and fury vibrated through me. It was the kind of anger I didn't know what to do with.

Her house was burning to the fucking ground.

I slowed my bike as I approached. A crowd had formed outside as the fire department worked hard to control the flames. From what I could figure, though, the fire was too intense. Hailee's home and all her belongings would be ash soon.

It fucking killed me that she would have to go through this. And that Jean would have to as well. Hailee had so much on her plate. Adding more shit to deal with would only cause her distress she didn't deserve.

I found a place to leave my bike and made my way through the crowd so I could talk with the firies. As I surveyed the damage, I clenched my fists. *The motherfuckers who did this would fucking pay.*

Chapter Twenty-Five

Devil

Hailee burst into tears when I finally arrived at the clubhouse a couple of hours later. After I'd spent some time talking with the firies, I tried to salvage anything I could from her house. In the end, though, nothing had been salvageable. I'd turned up at the clubhouse with nothing but bad news.

Clinging to me, she said, "Who would do this?"

"I don't know, darlin'. I suspect it's tied to what happened to your brother this morning." I'd filled her in on everything while watching the fire destroy the house. I was fucking thankful I'd told her to leave earlier that morning.

Nitro joined us. "Have you heard from King yet? I thought he'd be back by now. Or at least that we would have had a call."

I shook my head. "No, nothing."

"What about Hyde?"

"No." My anger and frustration with him had morphed into concern. With everything that had happened that day, I fucking hoped Hyde was okay.

"Fuck." He rubbed the back of his neck, and I saw the concern he held, too. "Okay, I'm gonna take care of upping our security. Let me know the minute you see or hear from King or Hyde, yeah?"

"Will do, brother."

Hailee stepped out of my embrace after Nitro left. Wiping her face, she said, "Gran's devastated. All our family photos and things are gone. I don't care about my stuff, but I hate that she's lost everything."

I curled my hand around her neck and pressed a kiss to her forehead. "I'm sorry, baby." There wasn't anything else I could say to ease her pain. "Where is Jean?"

"Kree organised for her to lie down in your room. I hope that's okay. She didn't think you'd mind."

"Yeah, that's good." I frowned. "Have you heard from Bronze?"

"Bronze?"

"Shit, Aaron."

"You call him Bronze?"

"Yeah."

She stared at me in silence, and I couldn't get a read on her. Not since she'd discovered Bronze was dirty. She'd been quiet after he and I fought the night before, but thank fuck she hadn't pulled away from me.

Finally, she placed her hand on my chest and said softly, "I feel like the biggest bitch."

That came out of left field. "Why?"

Tears fell down her cheeks again, and she madly wiped them away. "I was awful to him last night. It's none of my business what he chooses to do with his life. I mean, that's what I hate about my mother—the way she thinks she has a right to judge my choices in life."

I smoothed her hair. "I didn't think you were judging him so much as trying to come to terms with learning something new about him."

She swallowed a sob. "What if"—her hand flew to her mouth—"he'd been beaten to death this morning? I wouldn't have had a chance to tell him I love him always, regardless of what he does."

I moved one hand around her waist and the other around her back, and pulled her close. "He knows that, baby."

She buried her face against my chest, nodding while the tears flowed. I heard her sobs. Deep in my fucking bones, I heard them. She might have struggled at first to understand her brother's choice, but that she'd realised his choice in life wasn't a reason to withdraw her love was something about her I fucking respected. I fell for Hailee even more than I already had because of the way she loved unconditionally.

The moment was broken between us when King's voice bellowed from the doorway of the clubhouse bar. "This is fucking war!"

I turned to find him stalking my way, a look of complete fury on his face. "The motherfuckers set fire to my place, too. And Bronze's." His face softened a little as he glanced at Hailee and said, "We've also had word that the place you worked at was targeted. Bronze is working to get me more info, but so far he's advised me that a few of the staff members have been taken to hospital."

Hailee's eyes widened with worry. "Are they okay?"

"I don't know."

Her body sagged against me as King's gaze met mine. "We need to talk, brother." His meaning wasn't lost on me. We had to talk privately.

I nodded, my own fury still churning. "Give me a minute."

After he left us, I tipped Hailee's face up to mine. "We're going to find who did this. And I promise you, they will regret what they've done." I meant every fucking word. No stone would be left unturned as far as I was concerned. And it seemed like King was on the same page.

"I need to call Leona."

"I've gotta go talk to King. You good here on your own?"

"Yeah, go."

I bent and kissed her before I left, wishing like fuck again, that I could take this burden from her.

I found King in his office, barking orders into his phone. He had his back to me. When he ended the call and turned to face me, I sucked in a breath at the level of crazy I saw in his eyes.

"That was Bronze. He's just talked with one of his informants," he said, and I knew by his deadly tone that I wouldn't like what he was about to tell me next. "It was Silver Hell. They discovered he's working with us and helped us against them. Their goal today was to target his family and me. Word is they're coming for the rest of us soon."

My insides twisted with hatred and a deep desire for vengeance. Heat burnt my skin and squeezed my heart, crushing it inside my chest. It twisted and clawed at me, leaving a toxic and bitter taste on my tongue. "They'll pay, King. For everything they've done to our club and our families, this time and all the other fucking times. If it's the last thing I ever do. They will fucking bleed for what they've done."

"Fuck." He hissed as he clenched his fists. "We've got a problem with that, brother. The fucking feds have eyes on us 24-fucking-7."

I stepped further into the office. "I know, but I'm telling you, I give no fucks. That's my woman's family they've messed with. And my club family." Hell wouldn't even be enough for anyone who fucked with my family. I wanted to destroy them. I wanted to fucking slaughter them, and I didn't fucking care what it took to do that. "I will fucking lay down and die for my family."

His breathing turned ragged as he nodded. "Okay. But you don't do this on your own. And we make sure there's no fucking survivors."

I exhaled a long breath. "Agreed."

***

The rest of the day passed in a blur. I set Hailee, Jean and Bronze up at my place. I'd been surprised when he agreed to stay with me, but he'd made it clear he was only doing it to make sure his family was safe.

Hailee had finally located her friend Leona late that afternoon. She'd been admitted to hospital with burns to her arms. Hailee had been worried about her friend having a miscarriage. Turned out, though, that Leona wasn't pregnant, which had been a huge fucking relief. Surprisingly, no one had died. Five of Hailee's work mates had been hospitalised, including Rachel. Hailee showed me how fucking big her heart was when she spent time visiting Rachel, even after Rachel had treated her so badly.

Just after midnight, Hailee fell asleep, giving me some time to think over the plans King and I had set in motion late that afternoon. Silver Hell wouldn't fucking know what hit them when we got started.

Chapter Twenty-Six

Devil

"Scott fucking Cole!" King greeted the president of the Brisbane chapter with a slap on the back early the next night when he entered the clubhouse bar.

"How are you, brother?" Scott asked, a look of concern in his eyes.

"Ready to get to work," King answered.

He'd called for reinforcements yesterday afternoon when we sat down with Hyde and Nitro to work out our plan of attack. After being MIA in the morning, Hyde had turned up when shit went down. I still had no fucking idea what was going on with him, but when all this was over I'd find out. With the feds' eyes on us, we knew we needed numbers. Scott had jumped at the chance to bring his members down to help.

"I managed to round up twenty-six members. That gonna be enough?" Scott asked.

"Yeah, that should do it," King said. "You bring Havoc? That crazy motherfucker gets shit done."

Scott nodded. "He's outside."

King motioned for Kree to pour drinks as everyone filed into the bar. Soon the room was chaotic as we all greeted each other. I hadn't seen some of the members in years.

Jason Reilly's gaze met mine with a grin. "Devil, brother. Long fucking time."

"Heard you got married," I said.

Before he could reply, King bellowed, "Drink up. We've got shit to do." He raised his glass and then drained it.

Drinks were passed around the room, and we all followed suit before breaking apart into the groups we'd been designated.

Each group consisted of about eight men, and we had six groups in total. Each would be leaving separately in an effort to distract the feds assigned to trail us. There were only so many cops to go around; our goal was to send them out with the first few groups of members who left. The last couple would be the members who would head over to Silver Hell's clubhouse.

Night had fallen by the time the first group left in a van just after nine. We'd received information from different sources that Silver Hell was celebrating what they deemed a victory at their clubhouse that night. We figured the party would be in full swing by the time we got there and that they'd be distracted enough for us to achieve our goal.

The next three groups left on their bikes. The last two groups were in vans, similar to the first one that left. Our plan worked when the feds followed the first three groups, leaving the last few to ride out undetected.

I was in the second van with King, Hyde, Nitro, Scott, Havoc and Kick. We travelled the first fifteen minutes in silence, until Havoc spoke.

"You're confident we can pull this off? With the helicopter."

Hyde, who was sitting across from him in the back of the van, nodded. "Yeah. Our pilot knows his shit."

"You've used him before?" Havoc asked.

"A few times for drops. Jacko's brother served with him. He's never let us down," Hyde said.

Havoc seemed happy with that answer. After that, we sat in silence again for the rest of the hour trip.

When we drew near the Silver Hell clubhouse, Kick slowed the van to ease it into the bush where we'd worked out we would park until the helicopter pilot had completed his task. It was far enough away to prevent us being injured.

Griff's voice crackled over the handheld radio. "We're in position. You?" He was with the other group of members in the third van positioned on the other side of the clubhouse.

"Good to go," King spoke into his radio.

The helicopter pilot's voice filtered through. "Two minutes for me."

Adrenaline flooded my body as I gripped my rifle.

I was ready.

Ready to finally annihilate the club that had caused us so much pain and loss.

Time ticked by slowly while we waited out the two minutes. My breathing slowed when the helicopter finally came into sight. I followed its lights and watched, with deep satisfaction, as it dropped a satchel bomb over the clubhouse. I couldn't see the bomb, but I knew it was there. And when it detonated forty-five seconds after it was dropped, I almost held my breath waiting for the fire that was our goal to blaze through the building.

"Go, go, go!" King roared into the handheld radio, and Kick drove the van out of the bush where we waited.

He planted his foot, driving like a mad-man to get us closer to the clubhouse. When he skidded to a stop, Scott yanked the back door open, and we all jumped out, rifles in hand.

Fanning out into a line, we stormed the perimeter, ready to shoot anyone who exited the building. The team led by Griff were doing the same thing on the other side.

Fire consumed most of the clubhouse and had begun to spread. We didn't have long before the police and firies would arrive, but the short time we did have would be spent making sure there were no survivors. Leaving with any Silver Hell members still breathing would not be fucking acceptable.

I met King's gaze as he raised his hand, giving the signal we all waited for.

It was time for vengeance.

My preference would have been to kill every last member by hand. I craved the deep fucking satisfaction that would give me. But our options were limited, and this was the best one. Burn the motherfuckers and riddle them with bullets to finish the job.

I stared at the fire engulfing the clubhouse. The lick of the flames, the smoke, the burning smell of our enemy and the scorch of heat that reached for me were all fucking gratifying. Knowing we were ridding the earth of these assholes and keeping our families safe from them was the best kind of knowledge. It would mean the difference between sleeping at night and tossing and turning at night with worry.

Once King had given the signal, we all lifted our rifles and fired into the clubhouse. Bullets sprayed the air, the sound deafening.

Taking them down was like a fucking hit of cocaine.

A rush.

A high unlike any other.

Euphoric.

The only thing that would kick that high into overdrive would be to hear their screams and to look into their eyes as their nightmares came to life.

Time slowed as we chased death. The hunt helped satisfy my desire for retribution, but it would never sate my hunger for their blood on my hands. I needed to touch it and see it ooze from their wounds. To know it would never run through their veins again. *To know it would never give them life again.*

Chaos played out in front of me. Members tried to flee the chaos we'd inflicted on them, but as fast as they sought escape, we took it from them.

Bullets, fire and blood collided.

Death beckoned.

And the sweet, sweet taste of victory was ours.

By the time Kick sounded the van horn letting us know we needed to get out of there, no more members stumbled from the wreckage of the fire. That should have felt good, but it didn't. I wanted more. A whole lot fucking more.

"Devil!" Scott's voice penetrated my thoughts.

I stopped firing my weapon and glanced at him. As I did that, I caught sight of someone running from the clubhouse. I ignored Scott and took aim again. As he came closer, I realised it was Dragon.

Fuck, yes.

I tasted blood.

I fucking felt it on my hands.

My body took over, and I moved towards him. I ran on automatic pilot, lowering my weapon as I got closer. He appeared unarmed and injured to the point of almost being unable to stand.

His clothes were torn and dirty.

Cuts and gashes covered his skin.

Blood painted his face and one arm.

He was fucked.

But not completely.

Not enough.

He had to die.

No fucking way was I leaving the Silver Hell president alive.

"Devil!" Scott yelled again, but I ignored him.

"You fucking cunts will pay for this!" Dragon roared as I drew close.

I pointed my rifle at him. "How do you figure that, asshole? Your club is all dead, and I'm the one standing here with a fucking rifle."

"You didn't kill everyone."

"Just fucking shoot him!" Scott called out from behind me, getting closer.

My finger hovered over the trigger, ready to squeeze.

The rush of victory shot through my veins again. The high was greater this time because I could see up close the devastation we'd caused.

My chest pounded with anticipation.

Dragon's death was so close.

And still it wasn't enough.

I needed my hands around his neck.

I hungered for the feeling of his bones crunching and snapping.

I wanted to make sure, with my bare hands, that he'd never hurt my family again.

I lowered my rifle as the first cop siren sounded in the distance.

"For fuck's sake," Scott yelled. "Fucking take him out, Devil, so we can get the fuck out of here."

The urgency and the frenzy and the rage in the air all smashed into me as I stared at the man who had caused so much of our pain. Wrath roared in my ears. It was time to end this madness.

"You're a fucking pussy." Dragon tried to provoke me, but I maintained focus.

He would die.

More sirens rang out in the night air.

I dropped my rifle and met Dragon's gaze. "You ready to meet your maker, Dragon?"

Evil glinted in his eyes. The kind of evil that would cause most people to shudder. I wasn't most people. I would fucking go to battle with evil and win. "Fuck you," he spat.

Red blurred my vision and I snapped.

I embraced my own evil.

I let it unfurl and roar out of me.

My fist connected with his face, knocking him backwards. He lifted his arms to defend himself, but my crazed need for his death meant his defence was useless. I kept the punches coming while he stumbled back a few times before I finally knocked him to the ground.

My breaths came hard and fast as I stood over him. He struggled to remain conscious and his head fell to the side. I slapped his face and barked, "Open your fucking eyes, motherfucker. I wanna see them when I take your last breath from you."

His eyes fluttered open and he stared up at me. "Fuck you," he said again, but he was fading.

I placed my feet either side of his body and crouched over him. Punching him hard in the face, I growled, "No, fuck you!"

I punched his face again.

And again.

Over and over.

Bone shattered.

Crunched.

And I finally had his blood on my hands.

I finally had the vengeance I thirsted after.

King's voice filtered into my consciousness as he shoved my rifle at me. "He's almost dead, Devil. Take your fucking rifle and finish him off so we can get the fuck out of here before the cops turn up."

I stayed crouched over Dragon's body, committing his mutilated face to memory. I traced the wounds with my eyes before splaying my hand over his face and storing the feel of his ruins in my mind.

When I was done, I stood and took a step back. Lifting my rifle, I squeezed the trigger and ended his shitty life.

Chapter Twenty-Seven

Hailee

I stared silently at the burnt remains of my home late the next afternoon, willing the tears not to fall. But as Devil put his arms around me and pulled me against his body, they cascaded down my cheeks.

"Fuck," I muttered, wiping them away. "I swore I wouldn't cry again today."

"Baby," Devil murmured against my ear, "cry. Let it out."

Gran joined us. She'd left to circle the property, but there really wasn't much to see. "It's just a building, child, and a few belongings. They're not the important things in life."

I sighed. "You're always so practical. Those things meant something to you. I'm sad you lost them."

She shook her head, dismissing what I'd said. "You mean something to me. Aaron means something to me. If I'd lost either of you in that fire, then I'd be sad. Things can be replaced."

It had been a long two days, and my emotions were all over the place. Between Aaron being beaten, losing our homes and belongings to fire, and Leona and my old workmates being hurt, I was close to tears all the time. My anger at the men who'd done this to us overwhelmed me, and I was thankful to have Devil and Aaron by my side helping me function. They'd explained why we'd been targeted and had also assured me that we were safe from it happening again. I didn't care what that meant—that those men had been dealt with, biker style. I only cared that we didn't have to worry about them ever again.

"You ready to leave?" he asked.

I nodded. "Yeah. You ready, Gran?"

She hobbled in the direction of the car, calling out, "Yes," as she went. I loved how she seemed to always be able to just get on with life. Some days I wished I was more like her.

Devil drove us back to his place, all of us lost in our own thoughts. I knew he had a lot on his mind, too. He'd told me that the people who burnt our houses down had been taken care of. I hesitated to ask him what that meant, but I had a good idea. And it didn't bother me. It felt just.

I wasn't hungry that night, but Devil insisted I eat. He cooked spaghetti, and I picked at it while he watched me with concern. After dinner, we set Gran up in the lounge room with her favourite TV shows and then did the dishes together.

Reaching for his hand once we finished the dishes, I said, "I'm sorry I'm so low today. I just need a day or two, and then I'll be back to my usual self."

Before I knew what was happening, he lifted me and sat me on the kitchen counter. Moving between my legs, he wrapped his arms around me and said, "Darlin', there's no rush. You take your time getting your head together. I'll be right here for whatever you need."

I wasn't sure what I'd done to deserve someone as amazing as Devil in my life. Smiling at him, I said, "You never did tell me how you got your nickname."

He grinned. "Weren't you meant to give me something in order to get that out of me?"

I returned his grin. It was infectious. "I've held up my end of the bargain. You wanted a drink with me, and I gave you that, so spit it out, bossman."

"King gave me my nickname. He said I could lead someone into temptation just as easily as I could cause destruction."

"The devil," I murmured.

He brushed a kiss across my lips. "Yeah." He let me go and placed his hands on my thighs. He then slid one hand under my dress, down to the inside of my thigh and along my leg towards my pussy. Meeting my gaze, he said, "I want you in a dress every day."

His demand caused an ache between my legs, and I spread them to allow him access.

He shook his head. "Not here. Jean might come in."

I lifted a brow. "And here I thought you loved sex in public." Not that I wanted my gran to walk in on us. In the heat of the moment, I'd forgotten that was a possibility, but I liked to play with him as often as I could.

"Darlin', there's a difference between fucking you in public and fucking you in front of your grandmother. I do have some standards."

My lips curled up into a smile as I slipped my arms around his neck. "In that case, we should move this to the bedroom."

He scooped me up and carried me into his bedroom, laying me out across his bed. He grabbed hold of my legs and pulled me towards him so that my ass was on the edge of the bed with my legs resting over his shoulders while he knelt in front of me. After he pushed my dress up, he slid my panties off and dropped them on the floor after pressing them to his face and inhaling my scent.

Bending his face to my pussy, he said, "I could live off your smell. It gets me so fucking hard." Taking hold of my ass, he licked along my pussy before sucking on my clit.

I threaded my fingers in his hair and scrunched a handful of it as I cried out, "Yes!" My back arched up off the bed, and I closed my eyes when his tongue slid inside me.

He groaned as he tasted me, pushing his tongue deeper inside while his mouth sucked me. Wave after wave of pleasure consumed me, and just when I thought I couldn't take any more, he stopped and growled, "Fuck, Hailee, I want to live between your legs."

I lifted my head and reached down so I could hook my hand around his neck. I pulled him to me, and he slowly made his way up my body, tasting my skin everywhere as he moved.

I was greedy for him, and as soon as he was close enough, I dragged his mouth to mine and kissed him. He grabbed one of my boobs and squeezed it hard enough that I cried out in pain. It was the kind of pain that felt good, though, and I begged him for more.

"You like that?" he demanded while squeezing my other breast.

I nodded, desperate for more. "Oh, God, don't stop," I pleaded.

Suddenly, he stopped everything and moved off me. Reaching for his button on his jeans, he undid it and yanked his zip down as fast as he could. His eyes never left mine while he did this. Moving back on top of me, he rasped, "Wrap your legs around me, darlin', and hold on tight. This is gonna be rough and dirty."

I did as he said while he sucked one of my tits into his mouth. I hardly had my legs secured around him before he slammed his cock as far into me as he could.

"Fuck," he roared, pulling out. Pushing back in, he forced himself deeper the second time, groaning as he did.

"Keep going," I urged when he stopped, resting inside me.

He sucked one of my nipples into his mouth and nipped it with his teeth before looking up at me. "Tell me how you want me to fuck you."

Running my fingers through his hair, I said, "I want you to let loose. Forget everything in the moment and be an animal. I want it to hurt a little, but the kind of hurt that feels so fucking good."

"Fuck, woman." He drew my other nipple into his mouth and bit it harder, eliciting a cry of pain from me. Meeting my gaze again, he said, "You want it to hurt like that?"

I nodded. Oh, God, how I wanted it to hurt like that.

He moved fast then, rearing back so he could flip me onto my stomach. Scooping his hands around my hips, he pulled my ass up so I was bent at the waist with my head down, elbows on the bed holding me up. He gripped my hips tightly and positioned himself behind me, then pushed his cock inside.

Fuck.

I loved it when he took me from behind. And he knew it. He especially knew how much I loved him pulling my hair. But this time, he didn't stop to reach for my hair. He did exactly what I'd asked him to do, and fucked me like a savage while holding my hips, his fingers digging in hard.

After we were finished, I collapsed on the bed. Unable to move and fighting to catch my breath, I was spent. Devil crashed next to me, his body curling around mine, his arms holding me close. We fell asleep like that, and while I was emotionally wrecked by the events of the last two days, I felt protected by him.

I felt like I was exactly where I was meant to be.

Chapter Twenty-Eight

Devil

"From what I can work out, and from what Bronze has reported back to me, we got every last one of those motherfuckers last week," King said during Church the week after we destroyed the Silver Hell clubhouse and everyone in it.

"So that means we're down at least one enemy," Hyde continued. "Next on the list is Marx. After that, when the feds are done with him, we take down Gambarro." He glanced around the packed room. "People need to be reminded that Storm isn't to be fucked with."

Cheers erupted at that, but King kept the meeting moving. "Ghost has also been dealt with, so he won't be an issue going forward. And"—he eyed me—"I've sorted Bronze out, too. He's committed to the club again."

Once he'd caught everyone up, he discussed other club business that needed taking care of. Twenty minutes later, everyone filed out except for Hyde, Nitro, and me.

Looking at King, I asked, "How the fuck did you get Bronze back on side?"

"I pointed out that he could walk away from the club all he liked, but it wouldn't sort his problem out with you dating his sister."

I was still confused. "How?"

"He's got no dirt on you, Devil, no evidence of anything you've done. So even if he tries to bring the club down, you're still free to be with his sister."

"Jesus, he must have been pissed off about that."

"Yeah, he wasn't too happy, but it's sorted out now."

"How's Kick?" Nitro asked. "You heard any more from him about Evie?"

"Yeah, the doctors are keeping her in hospital. Possibly for the rest of her pregnancy depending on her blood pressure. Kick seems to think they might deliver the baby early. But he said she's doing well besides that. He's coming back tomorrow."

"Thank fuck," Hyde murmured, as if it was important to him that Kick was returning.

King picked up on it, too. "What's going on, Hyde?"

Hyde took a moment to reply. He seemed reluctant to answer the question. "I'm going to need some time off."

"Why?"

"I've got some family stuff I need to take care of."

King rubbed the back of his neck. He appeared frustrated. "What family stuff? I've always been under the impression you didn't have any family, Hyde. You've been all over the fucking—"

"It's my wife."

We all stood in shocked silence. I was certain none of us had seen that coming.

"You've got a wife?" King asked. "I've known you for fourteen years, and you've never once mentioned a wife."

"Yeah, a wife. A daughter, too."

"Fuck, Hyde. Why haven't you ever told us about them?"

Hyde seemed uncomfortable discussing this, but he forced himself to continue. "I haven't seen them for fourteen years." His voice dropped when he added, "But they need me now, and I need to do this. I know the timing is shitty, but—"

King cut him off. "No, you should go. Family is important. When will you be back?"

"I don't know. It depends on whether they accept my help."

“Okay, now I’m really fucking confused,” King said. “Why wouldn’t they?”

Hyde took a deep breath, and when he answered King, I heard emotions in his voice I’d never heard from him before, mostly regret and anguish. “They think I’m dead.”

Epilogue

Devil

3 months later

"Kylie! Adam! Uncle Dom is here," Sonya yelled out as I stepped through the front door of her house, before I'd even had time to say hello to her.

I chuckled. "Are they giving you hell today?"

She made a hand movement to signal she was pulling her hair out. "Like you wouldn't believe. Thank God you two are here now."

Hailee followed me in, laughing, too. Moving to Sonya, she embraced her and gave her a kiss on the cheek. "You're looking good, babe," Hailee said.

"I'll be looking a whole lot better after you and I get to the hairdresser next week, that's for sure. Is Leona coming with us? And how did your day go?"

"No, she's got an appointment with her doctor. She's finally pregnant! And my first day on the job was perfect." Hailee's investor had come through for her, and that day had been the grand opening of her massage charity.

The past three months had been tough on Hailee as she dealt with the fallout of the fire. She and Jean had moved in with me—temporarily at first, but then permanently when I pushed the point—but sorting out her work had been much harder. I'd felt the change in her today. The tension she'd been holding in her body had finally eased, and she seemed at peace with life again.

"That's fantastic news," Sonya said.

Hailee opened the fridge and found room for the caramel mud cake she'd made Sonya for tonight's dessert.

Sonya spotted it, her eyes lighting up. "Did you make me what I think you made me?"

Hailee grinned. "Yeah, your favourite."

Sonya made her way to where Hailee stood and threw her arms around her. Looking at me, she said, "The best day of my life was the day you met this woman. Don't ever make me have the worst day of my life, okay?"

"Fuck, no. I'm not planning on it."

From the minute I'd introduced the two women in my life, they'd bonded as if they were sisters. They had so much in common it wasn't funny. Some days I felt like I had to fight my sister-in-law to get time alone with my woman. But fuck, it was good to have family like this. Campbell still didn't have much to do with me, and I'd decided to finally face that my parents would never be what I wanted them to be, so Sonya, Hailee and Jean had become my family. I was still working on Bronze, but I was confident we'd bring him around one day. He loved Hailee too much not to accept me eventually.

The kids came running out, both of them throwing their arms around Hailee. I wasn't the favourite anymore. Not unless I turned up with presents.

"Auntie Hailee, come see my room!" Adam exclaimed, trying to drag her down the hallway.

As he pulled her away from us, Sonya mouthed, "Sorry."

My brows pulled together. "Why?"

She moved closer so she could speak softly. "I know you're always telling me to tell them not to call her that, but they love her so much they want her to be their aunt."

"It's all good. And it's not that I don't want them to call her that. I just never wanted her to feel pressured into it."

Sonya's eyes narrowed at me. "You say that like times are changing. Are they?"

I grinned as I pulled the ring out of my pocket and showed her. "Let's just say that I'm all for pressuring now. Four months together is long enough for a marriage proposal, right?"

"Since when does Dominic Ford care what anyone else thinks? And by the way, good fucking job on that ring. She's gonna love it."

"You reckon?"

She paused for a moment, assessing me. "What? Are you concerned she won't say yes?"

I scrubbed my hand over my face. "Fuck, I don't know. No. Yes. Fuck it, maybe."

She burst out laughing. "I never thought I'd see the day you were so pussy-whipped that you were actually nervous about what your woman would say."

"What is pussy-whipped?" Adam asked as he and Hailee stepped back in the kitchen.

Hailee's lips twitched, but she remained silent.

"Well," Sonya started, not seeming to know where to go after that.

Fuck it.

"It's me. I'm pussy-whipped, but you can't tell anyone, okay? It's our secret. Only we can know," I said.

His eyes glittered with excitement. Adam loved secrets. "Okay, I won't tell anyone."

Sonya started laughing again and muttered, "Oh, God, that's a classic, Dom."

My eyes found Hailee's. Unable to wait another second, I jerked my chin at her and said, "Get your ass over here, woman."

She lifted a brow. "Really? You're going all bossy on me today, Mr Pussy-Whipped?"

"Hailee," I said in the low warning tone I used on her when she was about to get her ass spanked. "I want to ask you something."

Sonya's head whipped around and she stared at me in surprise.

"Okay, how about we meet in the middle," Hailee said. "I'm not in a mood to be bossed today."

I took the few steps to meet her in the middle. Sliding my hand over her ass, I growled, "Always making me work for it."

Her smile lit the whole fucking room up. "Like I told you months ago, I've gotta keep you on your toes, bossman."

I bent my mouth to her ear. "And like I told you, I live on my fucking toes."

Her eyes sparkled. "Okay, what did you want to ask me?"

I shook my head. "No, I've changed my mind. I'm not asking. I'm bossing. And you're not saying no to me."

"Oh, really?" She gave me the look she reserved for when she was about to dig her heels in on something I wanted that she didn't want to give.

I pulled the ring out of my pocket again and reached for her hand. Sliding it on her ring finger, I said, "We're getting married. At the end of next month."

I heard her sharp intake of breath.

I saw her eyes water.

And then I felt her mouth on mine, kissing me in the way she did when I'd done something she really liked.

When she ended the kiss, she squealed louder than I'd ever heard anyone squeal. Flashing her ring at Sonya, she screamed, "We're getting married! You're stuck with me now, Sonny!"

I watched in amusement as the two of them hugged for much longer than she kissed me. Crossing my arms over my chest, I said, "Should I be jealous of my own sister-in-law?"

Hailee moved back to me and threw her arms around me. "I love you so damn much. In fact, I think I fell in love with you on our first date. I have eyes for no one but you, not even for Sonya."

I tightened my hold on her. "Baby, I fell in love with you in the back of that cop car. You were sitting there yabbering on about fucking greyhounds and gambling and fuck knows what else, and I knew you were the woman for me."

"How did you know?"

I grinned. "Because for the first time in my life, I wanted to talk to a woman more than I wanted to get in her pants. I would have sat there all fucking day listening to you talk about dogs."

Her face lit up. "And I would have jumped your bones if you'd have asked me to."

I brushed a kiss across her lips and said, "Marry me, darlin'."

She smiled. "I thought you'd never ask, bossman."

Acknowledgements

It's been three years since I published my first book. Back then, I never envisioned what the future of my writing career might be. I certainly didn't imagine the success I've had in the publishing industry. To say it takes a tribe to publish a book is the absolute truth. I owe thanks to so many people.

First and foremost, I am so very thankful to my readers who continue to buy my books and love my stories and characters. Without you, I wouldn't have a publishing career. Thank you for allowing me to do the only job I want to do. I feel so blessed to be able to spend my days writing.

Secondly, thank you to everyone who has ever helped me promote my books. Bloggers, readers and fellow authors—I love you so much for your amazing support.

I couldn't do this job without my assistant, Jodie O'Brien. She's been on this crazy ride with me for nearly two years and really is the Levine in all this. Thank you, PhanieWit, I love you so damn much and am more than blessed to have you in my corner. I will *always* be in yours.

I had two people help me with this book that I truly could not have done it without. Jodie is one. My editor, Becky Johnson is the other. At a time in my life when shit was falling down all around me, Becky stepped in and took my stress away. I love working with you, Becky and am so thankful that Jodie suggested I work with you. You won't ever get rid of me *insert evil laugh* OH, and I'm looking forward to building the *Nina Levine Biker Dictionary* with you ;)

There were times when I didn't think this book would come together. More than during any other book I've written. I received some devastating family news a few months ago and at that point I almost postponed the Sydney Storm series so I could spend time with my family. I decided to carry on as best I could. But writing a book when your mind is struggling to deal with your mother's illness, and while you're watching her get sicker and sicker, was way harder than I ever imagined it would be. Right up until the final week, I still wasn't sure I could pull it off. It's in those dark moments that you realise just what you're capable of. But honestly, if not for Jodie and Becky, I would have collapsed in a heap and given up. And I also have the amazing support of my Levine's Ladies group that helped get me through. I am so thankful for the many wonderful friendships I have found in that group.

I also have my beautiful friend, Chelle Bliss. She's there for me, always. Thank you, Chelle. Your friendship means so very much to me.

I must also give huge thanks to my cover designer, Letitia, and the photographer who shot the image of Jase Dean on the cover of this book, Wander Aguiar. Wander and his assistant Andrey have been absolutely amazing to work with and I am so in love with the images I selected for Devil's, Kicks, Hyde's and King's books. Thank you to both of you for making this an effortless task. And Letitia. My beautiful Letitia. *sigh* You did good, girl. Really fucking good. These are my favourite covers ever and I am so thankful to you for the way you work with me, never getting frustrated with me, and designing spectacular covers that not only I love, but that my readers adore, too.

To my beautiful daughter Eliahn, my BAE (yeah, I call her that because she's a teen and that's how we talk lol), you constantly amaze me with the things you do for me. You'll possibly never read this, but if you do I want you to know that none of my books would ever have been finished without you helping me. The way you take over the housework, shopping and cooking when it's deadline time gives me the space to create. The way you listen to all my crazy plot ideas and roll your eyes at them and tell me they suck and that they aren't original and that they are cliche... yeah, even that means the world to me. You, my gorgeous girl, are going to go far in this world and I'm so looking forward to the ride with you while you do it. Love you.

About The Author

Dreamer.
Coffee Lover.
Gypsy at heart.
Bad boy addict.

USA Today Bestselling Aussie author who writes about alpha men & the women they love.

When I'm not creating with words you will find me either creating with paper, paint & ink, exploring the world or curled up with a good book and chocolate.

I love Keith Urban, Maroon 5, Pink, Florida Georgia Line, Bon Jovi, Matchbox 20, Lady Antebellum and pretty much any singer/band that is country or rock.

I'm addicted to Scandal, Suits, Nashville, The Good Wife & wish that they would create a never-ending season of Sons of Anarchy.

I'm thankful to have found amazing readers who share my alpha addiction and love my story writing style. I'm also thankful that many of these readers have become friends. The best thing in the world is finding your tribe.

www.ninalevinebooks.com

Made in the USA
Monee, IL
31 January 2021

59099772R00146